HIGHWAY TO YOUR DREAMS!

How to make your dreams come true!

A personal account of a man fulfilling a dream by running across Oklahoma along historic Route 66!

By Steve Kime

xulon
PRESS

July 17, 2003

To: JOANIE,

Dream Big!

My best to you!

— Steve Kino

Isaiah 40:31

What people are saying about the book!

"What a fantastic book! Steve Kime is a powerful Keynote Speaker/Author and life-long runner who dedicated his dream to run across Oklahoma to benefit the Special Olympians of the great Sooner State. Read and more importantly, follow Steve's P.L.A.N. which outlines and assists you, so you too can make your dreams come true."

> Kevin Saunders
> *Paralympian, Former World Champion/Multiple World Record Holder. Was first person with a disability appointed to the President's Council on Physical Fitness & Sports by President George H. Bush, Senior Member for 2 terms under the Clinton Administration.*

"Most successful men I know are highly driven. They have a "special" motor that runs with high RPM's (Right Personal Motives). That usually equates to unselfish service to others. That, to me, describes this book. We are all called to live life to it's fullest. Let this book challenge you to be all you can be by choosing to live an abundant life."

> Chuck Bowman
> *CEO/Director of Development—
> Fellowship of Christian Athletes*

IN MEMORY OF MOM

TABLE OF CONTENTS

DEDICATION

This book is dedicated to Mom, Dad, Judy and Kak. Thank you for teaching me how to run! And it is dedicated to all my friends and athletes at Special Olympics of Oklahoma.

FOREWORD

What you are about to read is the story of a man who ran. I first met Steve Kime at a Special Olympics luncheon. Steve was the keynote speaker for the event and he shared an inspirational story of his run 13 1/2 miles up to the Summit of Pikes Peak in the Colorado Rockies.

I remember a story that Steve shared that day about how a "grandma" passed him during the run up the mountain and while she was passing Steve she said, *"Come on Okie, you can make it! Come on Okie, you can make it!"* Steve said those words came at a time when he needed a word of encouragement to reach the Peak! Steve said that he would never have reached the Summit if it hadn't been for those words of encouragement. In my opinion, this book will encourage you to reach for your dreams.

Steve is a Sooner. He was born in Perry, Oklahoma home of the Maroons and he was born to run! I met up with Steve again at the annual Special Olympics Summer Games. This time he looked a little different. Steve had just completed his 397-mile run across Oklahoma along historic Route 66. He did this all because of a dream. A dream that wouldn't go away. A dream to run across the Sooner State in an effort to bring awareness to the programs of Special Olympics Oklahoma.

We both have one thing in common. And that is a passion for Special Olympics Oklahoma. We have a passion in supporting the many athletes that pursue their dreams through the year-round sports training and athletic competition programs. This book isn't just about running. It's about pursuing your dreams. The book tells you how to put a plan in place to experience your dreams! Steve Kime is known as a professional speaker with a message of encouragement. This book will encourage you! So, tie the laces on those running shoes and get ready to run! And run in the direction of your dreams!

Coach Barry Switzer
Former Head Football Coach Oklahoma Sooners and Dallas Cowboys

ACKNOWLEDGEMENTS

For their encouragement throughout my life and support of this project, I will always be grateful:

- To Casey, my daughter, for being such a joy in my life.
- To Randy Ellis for encouraging me to take the first step. Randy, your run across the United States made me realize my run across Oklahoma was a "walk in the park!"
- To Mary and Bud Butler for giving of their time and talents to be the best support team in the world. Thanks to you both for making this venture so successful and memorable. You were the best support team anyone could ask for.
- To Dan Miyoshi for coming all the way from Las Vegas to join the support team. Dan thanks for always handing me the right things at the right time.
- To all my Special Olympics friends who gave me the opportunity to live my dream. Thanks to Adrian DeWendt, Lynn Gillis, Kathy Wise, Jennifer Polay and John Seals.
- To Carol and Mike Brumley for seeing me safely to the Kansas border. Remember, "See you on down the road Jack!"
- To Paul Mabrey for encouraging me to "just do it!"

- To Lt. Governor Mary Fallin for your support of Special Olympics Oklahoma.
- To John Swasho and Kimball Davis for running with me on those long training runs.
- To all the law enforcement agencies in Oklahoma that provided protection from the traffic and big dogs. I couldn't have made it without your escorts.
- To my dear brother Dr. David Dyson for being on the end of the phone at all times.
- To Betty Casey and Judi Mills for being another set of eyes for this project.

AUTHOR'S NOTE

Dear Reader:

I believe the story line of the movie *Forrest Gump* spoke to the hearts and minds of millions who watched this box office smash . It seemed when Forrest met people, he innocently touched their life in a special way. Tom Hanks' portrayal of an man with an unconditional spirit who ran across the United States for three years, two months, fourteen days and sixteen hours helped place a fire within my heart that continues to burn today. That fire encourages me to run.

This book is the product of running 397 miles across the State of Oklahoma in 16 days. It is also the result of my running days starting back in Perry, Oklahoma many years ago. I have had the privilege of running in foreign countries, to the Summit of Pikes Peak in Colorado, across the desert of Death Valley and through Arlington National Cemetery at sunrise early morning. My most enjoyable run was when I ran into many individuals who have made a lasting impression upon me. My hope is for this book to be a source of encouragement for you to Live the Dream. I'm reminded of a quote that is found on the gravestone of Eric Liddell. Eric was the character inspiration for the movie *Chariots of Fire.* The inscription on the stone reads,

> *"We enter the starting blocks of life not knowing the length of the race. Our life may be a marathon or a sprint – we are not told in advance. All we can decide is how we will run the race."*

Please join me in a run across the Sooner State down the Mother Road Route 66. We will race through the pages of this book and begin building a plan to live our dreams. So, let's run together down the highway to your dreams!

Chapter One

BILL'S CORNER

There is a four-way intersection in north central Oklahoma were the highways of 64 and 77 meet. It is known to many Oklahomans as Bill's Corner. The intersection is nothing spectacular. It does have an old abandoned gas station that's been there since day one. I haven't met Bill, and don't know if there even was a Bill, but I do know that from a very early age, that intersection had a special name.

I grew up in Perry, Oklahoma, which is exactly 12 miles west of Bill's Corner. In the summer of 1971, I decided to run from my house on the eastern edge of Perry to Bill's Corner. I had driven the stretch to this four way stop many times, but never ran the 12 mile distance. I thought it a nice challenge since I never heard of anyone from Perry running the distance. I remember mentioning to my high school track coach that I was going to run all the way to Bill's Corner. I recall he asked my why, but that was about it for a response. He said, *"Why spend the time and effort to do such a thing?"*

I admit I didn't do a good job expressing to my coach why I was running. There seemed to be an inner voice calling me to run! For a seventeen-year-old boy, it was difficult to communicate the rationale for running this distance. Little did I know that running those 12 miles to Bill's Corner was really following one of my first dreams. A dream to run the distance just so I could say I ran all the way to the Highway 64-77 intersection.

To the northwest of Bill's Corner were some farm implements and the beginnings of a wheat field. Pasture land lay to the southeast and an abandoned building stood on the southwest corner. The old building looked at one time to be a grocery store so Bill's Corner was no tourist attraction. Just a four-way stop for those traveling north to Ponca City, east to Morrison, south to Stillwater and west to Perry.

I left my house at 7:00 a.m. on a weekday morning. I wasn't sure how long it was going to take to run the 12 mile distance, since the longest I had run at that time was a couple miles. I was a middle distance runner in school, so this was new frontier for me. Still, it was a dream and desire to go the distance. At the four mile mark I was running past the home of Ashley Alexander. Ashley, a noted musician and teacher at Perry Schools and Oklahoma State University lived on the Bill's Corner route. I have known Ashley Alexander all my life. I would see him on Sunday mornings at the bench of the church organ playing away! I always admired his faithfulness to play the organ for our church and I admired his tremendous musical talents. As a young person I remembered Ashley as the individual who would travel the state and perform musical concerts. I believe he could play every instrument invented. Ashley is still the only guy I know who can carry on a conversation with you, shake your hand, while playing the church organ at the same time. He truly never missed a beat! Mr. Alexander knew I was a runner and we would occasionally talk about my high school track accomplishments, of course he was pounding those black and white keys during our visit. My friend was so gifted and had a warm smile that you could never forget.

I was running alongside the road of Highway 64 heading east and I saw Ashley in his front yard. At first he just waves and smiles. Then, with a confused look, he does a doubletake and stares as I just wave and keep on running. Ashley continues to smile and shake his head in disbelief. Keep in mind, I'm miles out of city limits from where I should be and Ashley sees this 17-year-old kid running by. I did try to exhibit some type of confidence that I knew what I was doing for those 12 miles. A stray dog or even a hitchhiker on Highway 64 isn't uncommon, but a 17 year old kid running is uncommon. I finally arrive at Bill's Corner a couple hours later. It was a warm summer morning in Oklahoma and after a dozen miles I was feeling the heat.

I arrived at Bill's Corner within a few hours and just stood there looking around. No welcoming committee or fanfare. No finish line with people in the stands. No one really even noticed I was there. Just a four-way stop with cars passing through. Motorists looked at me with curiosity and seemed to be asking what is this guy doing? This is a rural area and a guy wearing running shorts and dripping with sweat looks a little out of place. I walked over to the service station and waited for my friend, Johnny Rogers who promised to give me a ride back into Perry. Johnny was no where in sight. I waited a few minutes and decided to visit with the service station manager to explain my dilemma. He didn't offer any suggestions to get back to Perry, but did allow me to go and stand underneath the water hose to cool off. I can still remember that refreshing feeling 31 years later. Whew! That water was cold!

I ran 12 miles. I proved to myself that I could do it. Now what? Since my friend Johnny wasn't there, I decided to walk back to Perry. I knew I was not supposed to hitchhike but I didn't have the strength to run another 12 miles back into town. I started walking along Highway 64 and within a couple miles Johnny appeared saying he overslept. I didn't care what his excuse was, I was just glad he is there to give me a ride. Arriving at home was uneventful. Only Johnny, my track coach, Ashley and my mom even knew that I had run the distance. That was okay with me. It was something that I had to do!

What's the big deal about running to Bill's Corner? For several months I had this thought, inspiration or mental challenge to run the 12 miles. I dreamed about running this distance. Since I wasn't aware of anyone from Perry running to Bill's Corner, the dream became more of a challenge. I dreamed about what it would take to run such a distance. I dreamed about what the finish would feel like. It was a dream that I had to act upon. I realize that a 12-mile run in today's world is not a significant achievement to some. But to a soon-to-be 17 year old high school senior in 1971, it was a big deal! It was a chance to live the dream! It even gave my friend Mr.

Alexander and me something new to talk about. For many years to follow, we would talk about that moment when we exchanged smiles and wave of hand as I ran by his house.

Today, every time I drive through that intersection the memories of the morning run come back to me. The traffic, the heat of the summer morning sun, Ashley waving at me with a look of wonder, and of course, that icy cold water from the hose at the service station. More importantly, I'm reminded of the dream set before me 31 years earlier. I'm reminded of the chance to fulfill the dream to go the distance. When I pass through the four-way stop, I'm reminded of all those experiences of the run and peace, satisfaction and fulfillment come to me all because I acted upon the dream. Running the distance proved to me that I could live the dream. Little did I know that this lesson set the stage for living future dreams!

Running 12 miles to Bill's Corner was more than just arriving at a four-way stop. It was about accomplishing a dream. A dream that was entirely mine. It might not make sense to anyone else, but that's okay, it was my dream. Bill's Corner is just an intersection for people to pass through on the way to their destination. Years later, I realized that running those 12 miles gave me the confidence I needed to move forward to new destinations. Running to this place in the road was about doing something that I hadn't done before. It felt good to live this dream.

Let me ask you a question. What is your Bill's Corner? What is your dream? It doesn't have to make sense. It can be whatever you want. What dream is in your mind and heart that will not go away? If I can run to Bill's Corner, then you can experience your dream!

In this book we will explore ways to live our dreams. Bill's Corner was just a prelude to my 397-mile run across the State of Oklahoma along Route 66. This book is about my dream to run west to east across the Sooner State. So here we go! Let's get a plan in place to Live Our Dreams!

It was Plato who said, '*the beginning is the most important part of the work.*"

Chapter Two

THE DREAM

I placed a call to my friends Adrian DeWendt, Executive Director of Special Olympics Oklahoma and Paul Mabrey. Paul was the Development Director of Special Olympics Oklahoma at that time and had been helpful in previous "Forrest Gump" runs benefiting Special Olympics. I had a great working relationship with these two individuals, but wasn't quite sure how they would handle the news I was about to share with them.

One March morning, as I sat in Adrian's office with he and Paul, I hesitantly shared my dream. I wanted to make a good impression upon these two guys, but what I was about to share with them might shatter the confidence they had in me. The dream was about me dressing up like Forrest Gump, and running across the State of Oklahoma along with Special Olympic athletes. In my dream, I am dressed in a plaid shirt, khaki pants, a bright red Bubba Gump Shrimp baseball cap and of course those white Nike shoes with the "red swoosh." No mistake here, this was my dream. Every night for two months, I would fall asleep and then like a videotape playing in my mind, I would relive running across the state with my Special Olympians by my side. Night after night the same dream. I never knew where I was. I didn't know if I was running through Texola, Elk City, or Tulsa. But I could see in my mind's eye the vision of simply running across the Sooner State.

I shared the entire dream with my Special Olympic friends and summed it up by saying, "You know gentleman, I think I'm supposed to run across the state."

And with that, Adrian and Paul said, "Well let's make a plan."

Chapter Three

RUNNING ACROSS KANSAS

Before the run across Oklahoma my friend Suzanne Fitzgerald Wallis encouraged me to run across the state of Kansas on Route 66. Suzanne and her husband Michael are both noted experts on the subject of Route 66 in which Michael has written a book entitled: *Route 66 – The Mother Road.* I was visiting with Suzanne one day in her office asking for her input into the best way to run across the state on what's known as the Main Street of America.

Suzanne suggested as a tune up, "Why don't you run across Kansas?" My first reaction was one of astonishment. I don't have the legs or strength to run Kansas and then Oklahoma. Suzanne explained to me that Route 66 cuts through the southeast corner of Kansas. Thirteen miles of Kansas land separates Missouri from Oklahoma. I thought, this I can do!

On November 25, 2000 I participated in the Seventh Annual Race Across Kansas and, dressed up as Forrest, I ran from the Missouri border through Galena, Kansas all the way to Baxter Springs on the Oklahoma border. That was a very cold Saturday, but with all the media attention from the Kansas newspaper reporters and television stations from Joplin, Missouri, it warmed my heart. It gave me an opportunity to share the reasons I run dressed in character and the important role Special Olympics plays in the lives of many individuals. I dressed as Forrest because he is one of my favorite movie characters but being dressed differently from the "real" runners gives me a platform to speak from. I run to bring awareness of Special Olympics.

Special thanks to Darrel Ray and Scott Nelson for inviting me to participate in the annual event which marked the beginning of many exciting events.

Now it was time to set my sights on the Sooner State. Time to create a plan!

Webster's Dictionary defines a plan as "a formulated scheme for getting something done." So we began putting a plan together, a plan that would get me from Texola, Oklahoma at the Texas border all the way to Baxter Springs, Kansas just across the Oklahoma state line.

2001 was the year to celebrate the 75th anniversary of the existence of Route 66 also known as the Mother Road and Main Street of America. It seemed to be a perfect fit. I would run 397 miles across the state on the historic highway that was built to connect Illinois to California. My run would bring attention to both Route 66 and Special Olympics Oklahoma. The stretch of Route 66 across Oklahoma passes through 33 cities and covers more miles than the portions running through the other seven states of the Mother Road. I would run west to east across the state and recognized this was going to take a "good" plan to make it happen.

I don't want to overwhelm you with the numerous details that went into this event, but I want to summarize the efforts into four significant headings. The planning to make this "run across Oklahoma" a success would take many people from all walks of life and from various parts of the state and about one year's worth of preparation.

For the sake of the book I would like to share with you a simplified formula that was used. Narrowing down the PLAN to four steps doesn't minimize the amount of hard work that took place, but will help put a rather easy outline in place to begin using today. These four steps serve as an outline to make it happen. I'm using the word PLAN as an acronym to serve as our guide.

P stands for "**Prepare the Mind.**"

L stands for "**Listen to your Heart.**"

A simply means to "**Act on It**"

N is to remind us to "**Never give Up.**"

It was Stephen A. Brennan who said, *"Our goals can only be reached through a vehicle of a plan, in which we must fervently believe, and upon which we must vigorously act. There is no other route to success."*

Chapter Four

P—PREPARE THE MIND

I now use the P.L.A.N. format in my new motivational talk entitled: Living the Dreams! It's simple, easy to remember and I
think an outline to assist any individual in the pursuing of his or
her own dreams. Let's take a moment and look at this plan and see
how you can customize these steps into a plan of action for you.

The first step is: **Prepare the Mind**

If we have dreams we want to experience, we must ask this question: What is the dream going to cost me? What is required of me
to accomplish this task? What must I put in place to get going in
order to achieve this dream.

When we take a moment to count the cost this allows us to be in
a position to begin planning and to begin preparing the mind. Many
dreams may require physical efforts on our behalf, but our mind
must be just as prepared and up to the challenge. The Chinese
proverb, *"a journey of a thousand miles begins with a single step"*
began to take on a very realistic meaning to me as I formulated my
own plan to complete my run..

In preparation for my run across the state of Oklahoma, I took a
piece of notebook paper and answered some questions. What is this
going to cost me? It was going to take anywhere from 15-20 days

out of my normal lifestyle and require a physical effort of running about a marathon a day.

My friend Randy Ellis ran across the United States, running approximately 30 to 40 miles a day and sometimes further. He ran from California to North Carolina. Now, that's a run! After a couple of lunch visits with Randy to discuss strategy, I thought my body could easily handle 26.2 miles per day, a marathon a day. At this rate I would complete the run in two weeks time. While preparing the mind for the task at hand, I found it helpful to talk with individuals who have experienced a similar dream or achievement. As I mentioned, Randy had run across the United States in a matter of a few months and he chose Route 66 as his road of choice.

I recalled an old saying, *"Experience is the dividend gained from one's mistakes."* Randy's experiences and knowledge from his cross-country run was extremely valuable to me as I began preparing my mind, counting the cost and formulating my plan to run.

I calculated it would take approximately 2,096,000 steps to cover the 397-mile distance along Route 66. I calculated I would consume a minimum of seventeen gallons of water or sports drinks and over 80 power bars and all the food in sight. I'm always looking for my next meal, so it was difficult to estimate how much I would eat in one meal. I thought it would be everything.

I prepared for the heat, cold, fast cars, and pickup trucks with wide side mirrors. At times, I thought the challenge for drivers of pick up trucks was to see how close they could get with their mirrors. Even when I ran off the pavement and on to the shoulder. Overall, the majority of drivers moved over and were very accommodating.

Many days I would sing our state song, repeating the lyrics *"when the wind comes sweeping down the plains."* The wind was definitely a factor during the months of March and April. But running west to east along the Mother Road, most of the time the Oklahoma wind and rain blew across my path.

Since I prepared myself physically and mentally regarding food, water, and the weather, I felt all was in order. I had covered all the bases and nothing was left to do but run. I soon learned I had failed to prepare for one significant thing. Dogs. Do you realize Oklahoma has some of the biggest and fastest dogs in America? One impressive brown and black dog with big teeth resided just east of Weatherford and another very fast black dog lived in Commerce, home of Mickey Mantle. I want to say a special thanks to Officer Lt. Ray Harvey of the Commerce police department for his assistance. Officer Harvey headed that very mean dog off at the pass or in this case, Route 66.

Why am I taking the time in this book to talk about big dogs? Running across the state the memories of those brief and scary encounters with the dogs brought to mind an interesting point. I prepared for everything except being chased by dogs. As you prepare to live your dreams you too may have everything in order but might forget about the big dogs.

What are some of those big dogs you may face everyday? Maybe it's drugs, alcohol, or perhaps individuals in your life who may not be supportive of your dreams.

It's interesting, many people thought I was crazy to run 397 miles, but I surrounded myself with believers. The believers were simply people who believed in me and encouraged me to live out my dream. The best advice I can give anyone about confronting the dogs is run. Just keep running in the direction of your dreams!

When you find the answers to the questions I referred to earlier in this chapter, the fun begins. Excitement starts to build because you're one step closer to living the dream! So go ahead, find that someone that may have achieved a dream similar to yours and learn from their experience and knowledge. It will reduce the learning curve big time! It's time to prepare the mind!

According to Thomas R. Dewar, *"Minds are like parachutes; they only function when open."*

Chapter Five

L—LISTEN TO YOUR HEART

D o you hear it? I know many of you have heard it. Listen to that soft voice that keeps whispering to you. Day after day, night after night. It's the voice of encouragement. The voice that is saying live your dreams.

I'm reminded of the opening scene in the movie *Dead Poets Society* starring Robin Williams. Mr. Williams, who played the role as Mr. John Keating, was an English teacher at a prep school and brought his class full of young impressionable men to a large glass enclosed trophy case. The case contained years of athletic awards and student achievements. As he encouraged the young men to lean in towards the cabinet, he whispered softly the words as if they were coming from the trophies and photographs of students of years gone by. Whispering to them *"Car'pe Di'em, Car'pe Di'em, Car'pe Di'em."* As their mentor he said, can you hear it? Car'pe Di'em. Mr. Keating was trying to send a message to his young students to "Seize the Day." Don't wait any longer. Seize the Day!

As I shared in a previous chapter, every night for two months I dreamed. This is unique because it was the same dream each night. And it wouldn't go away. I would go to bed and upon falling asleep it was like someone would push play on my mind machine and play

33

the same tape over and over. I'm a slow learner so after one month of replaying this dream in my mind I started paying attention to what was being said.

The message was along the lines of "wake up, Steve, and start running." So here I am, in this dream dressed like Forrest Gump running across the state with Special Olympic athletes by my side. In the dream I envisioned myself running along a highway in wide-open spaces. There were pictures in my mind of wheat fields, pastures, and always the long straight highway in front of me. I couldn't recognize the Special Olympians running step by step with me in the dream, but there were many. I guess I had a vision similar to a scene in the movie *Forrest Gump* where Forrest is running across America with many people following. Of course this dream didn't make much sense to me at the time. But there was such a strong urge or message in the dream encouraging me to get busy running. It only took two months of dreaming the same dream over and over for me to get into action.

Here's one thought I don't want you to miss. The dream troubled me so much that I finally discussed it with Adrian and Paul. After that morning meeting and having a very productive day taking care of business, I was ready for a good night's sleep. Remember I'm expecting the dream to be replayed one more time just like the previous 60 days. Guess what? I didn't dream the dream again. It stopped. Someone pressed the stop button. Isn't that powerful? After I shared the dream and began putting a plan in place ... the dream stopped playing in my mind! To me, that was confirmation that I was on the right track. It only took 60 days to get my act together! I'm convinced that I would still be dreaming that dream a year later if I hadn't acted on it.

Victor Hugo once said, *"There is nothing like a dream to create the future."*

Do you have a dream that will not go away? There's a good chance the dream will keep speaking to you. You may have this dream for years, and it continues to whisper softly. It will continue to speak to your heart and mind. Don't discard the dream; just act on it.

I'm reminded of a popular quote by Henry David Thoreau who once said, *"If one advances confidently in the direction of his dreams, and endeavors to live the life which he has imagined, he will meet with a success unexpected in common hours."*

Today or tonight as you dream, let me whisper the words to you of Car'pe Di'em and encourage you to seize the day and your dream!

Chapter Six

A—ACT ON IT!

To this day, I am amazed at the impact the "stopping" of the dream had on me. You dream and think about a project for some length of time and it becomes a part of you. It can preoccupy your thinking and then all of a sudden it stops. I'm not sure if it happens this way for everyone, but I know it happened to me.

It was Paul Valery that said, *"The best way to make your dreams come true is to wake up!"*

Procrastination could be defined as a delay in action. There may be valid reasons to procrastinate but I think you will agree that putting off certain tasks can get us into trouble.

I was always told that *"tomorrow is often the busiest day of the week."* I don't think I was procrastinating regarding my dream, but was hesitant because it was so unusual. Which brings me to this point remember it's your dream, go for it! It may be strange or difficult to see in fruition, but again I think there is a sense of uniqueness in all dreams. I sincerely believe my dream gave me a glimpse of what was to come. Perhaps your dream will prompt you in the same way. You might get just enough insight into your dream that gets you excited and ready to take action.

There is a story about a young woman sitting in a chair by herself at an airport. The young woman is noticeably upset because of her crying and disheveled condition. A young couple on their way to their departure gate walks by the upset woman and has compassion for her and asks the question, "What is wrong?" The young woman said, "I can't find my ticket! I've looked in my bags, my coat and everywhere. I've lost my ticket and I don't have any money. I can't get home. What am I going to do now?" The caring young couple decided to offer assistance. The three of them looked around for the ticket and checked pockets on the coats and finally said to her, "Come with us over there to the snack bar and we'll buy you something to eat and figure out a way to get you home." Reluctantly, the woman gets up with the help of the young man. He grabs the woman's bags and large coat as the three of them begin to walk away. Suddenly, the young woman that has lost her ticket is screaming, and shouting with joy scaring the helpful man and wife. She said, "Look there's my ticket. I must have been sitting on it all the time."

Sometimes you and I have to "get up off our ticket" and "get home" so to speak. We may like the view sitting down but we're not getting anything done.

There's an old adage that says, "It's like sitting in a rocking chair. It gives you something to do, but you don't get anywhere."

The dream continues to speak. It's waiting for you to take action. It's waiting for you to get up off your ticket and act on it. It's alright that you don't know the outcome of the dream. Remember, "The journey of a million miles begins with the first step." This is the beginning of something exciting.

Go ahead take the first step. It's your dream. Time to act on it!

Chapter Seven

N—NEVER GIVE UP

Winston Churchill was noted as saying the words "N*ever, never, never give up*" in an address to the people of Great Britain. That statement contained more than a message from these powerful words. It was a declaration to the remind the world that the people of the United Kingdom were going to stand their ground no matter what the cost. These three words, "never give up," served a whole new meaning for me during my run across Oklahoma.

After two days of jogging, or 50 plus miles of Route 66 running, I developed some blisters and knee problems. For the record, I've never had problems with my feet or knees in all my years running. Jokingly, I tell people I've been running all my life. I ran from my mother when I got in trouble and I ran from the law (just kidding). Seriously, I can't remember a time that I didn't run. As a young boy I would rather run than take the time to walk somewhere. When I was in college running track I had a few aches and pains, but nothing too serious. So, when I developed blisters on the front, side and back edges of my feet along with "runners knee" also known as the iliotibial (IT) band syndrome, these injuries were quite a setback. This was a new frontier for me. I was always so blessed not to have any problems while running. Blisters and knee problems were the last thing I expected.

The blisters developed because of the crown in the road on Route 66. The Mother Road had a slope to it allowing rainwater to run off efficiently during storms. I expected to have a few problems with the feet, but believe me, from all the years running I have some callused feet. With the slope of the road, my feet would slide to the side of my shoe causing additional friction. When you're doing 25 plus miles a day, even with rest, there might be a chance of blisters showing up.

I had four pairs of shoes to alternate during the run, plenty of good socks and all the precautions needed to avoid blisters. Despite my preparation, the blisters got so bad that my feet bled continously. The blistered skin was so raw that it is difficult to describe in words the amount of discomfort and PAIN I encountered. But I couldn't quit!

It's interesting how news travels. By the time I reached the State Capital at Oklahoma City, the television media was more interested in taking pictures of my bloody feet and blisters than talking to me about the run across the state. After the interview aired on the 5 o'clock edition of one station, I talked to my dad on the phone while running and he commented, "Nice size feet, Steve. Oh, by the way, nice size blisters too."

I was fortunate to meet an athletic trainer from the University of Southwestern Oklahoma at a speaking engagement in Weatherford and he graciously gave me a quick exam. After a few painful pushes on the knee he said, "You have a problem with the IT band." In layman's terms it's called runners knee. This band is a group of fibers that run along the outside of the thigh. IT Band, runner's knee, or iliotibial band syndrome, all I know is that along the outside of my knee it really hurt to run. Basically, a tendon that runs down the side of the leg is a stabilizer during running, so when it's over-worked it causes excessive pain. I'm the first to admit my pain tolerance is slight, but this really did hurt. The joy of running was gone!

I share this medical condition information with you because I was in trouble. Emotionally I was defeated. What was I going to do? My body was saying, "you can't continue running." Physically, my feet and knees hurt and yet I had over 300 miles to go. Each running step I took was extremely painful. I kept thinking of all the people I would disappoint because I was unable to continue the run across Oklahoma. So many individuals were counting on me. So many cities were expecting me to run through their towns on specific dates.

I was enjoying a rather nice pity party with me, myself and I along Route 66 when I decided to call a dear friend.

Thanks to my Cingular Wireless friends who served as a run sponsor, I had a cell phone to call my friend Dr. David Dyson. I have always admired David for his wisdom and uncanny ability to say the right thing at the right time. As I was sharing my dilemma, and continued to enjoy my pity party, his strong confident voice on the other end uttered these words:

"Steve, the objective is the same, but the strategy has changed!" This may not sound profound to you but it hit me full force. The objective is the same. I can continue to work my way across the Sooner State, but the strategy had changed. I can now walk, skip, crawl, run, do whatever it takes to get across Oklahoma. You see, I had this mindset that I must run full stride every step of the way along Route 66. I guess I was caught up in the Hollywood story in which Forrest Gump ran continuously for years. I had the same expectation of running all the way full speed. Dr. Dyson helped me realize that I could still accomplish my goal of getting across the state, but my methodology of getting there could change. With that bit of encouragement from my friend, I continued to walk, run, jog along the Mother Road, which allowed my knees and blisters a chance to recover as I moved toward my goal.

How does this statement, "The objective is the same but the strategy has changed" have anything to do with you, the reader? Let me share this possible connection with you. I was the keynote speaker at a Management Conference and after making the "PLAN" presentation, which is about my run across Oklahoma, a young woman came up to me and shared her thoughts regarding that specific point about the objective and strategy.

She said, *"Steve, your story about how the strategy can change is so true. I got married to a healthy young man and we had dreams of doing so many things together. Soon after our wedding day my husband became ill and his health gradually deteriorated to a point that I must care for him 24 hours a day. He is confined to a bed or wheelchair most of the time. Our objective is still the same. To spend our lives together and enjoy each other every day, but the strategy has changed. We no longer are able to take trips and experience some of our outdoor travel dreams, so our strategy of doing things together has changed. Now we just focus on the objective."*

I was so moved by this woman's sincerity and willingness to be so vulnerable in sharing her story. I ask her permission to share the story and I hope it will be of help to you.

Helen Keller once said, *"We can do anything we want to do if we stick to it long enough."* Never give up! Remember, the objective is the same, but the strategy has changed."

Chapter Eight

YOU KNOW THE PLAN... GO THE DISTANCE

Have you ever had a song that plays over and over in your mind? You can't think of anything else but this song. Maybe you heard a particular song once and it never left your memory bank. Perhaps it was catchy tune and you just whistled it all day long. While running across the state, I had this song in my mind that wouldn't go away. Not sure where it came from, but it played continuously during the time spent out on the road.

In the Walt Disney motion picture *Hercules,* the theme song in the movie sung by Michael Bolton was entitled: *Go the Distance.* That song kept playing over and over in my mind when running along Main Street of America. I must have heard it on the radio because I never did see the movie. For some reason, the inspirational tune just took hold in my mind. I didn't know the words to the song, but I could hum rather impressively and then say the words "Go the Distance." Now that I think about it, it's a good thing that I didn't start singing *Running on Empty* by Jackson Browne. Through the aches and pains, the blisters, dodging traffic, wind and rain, hot and cold temperatures, the words "Go the Distance" became my theme. These three words served as inspiration for me. The words had some type of encouraging power that would "kick-start" my engines every morning. No matter what came my way, I was going the distance!

As you go the distance with your dreams, remember to draw upon the many sources of strength and encouragement available to you. During my 16 day run, I drew upon the strength of my support team. Bud, Mary, Dan, Carol and Mike were the best crew anyone could assemble. They were always there with an encouraging smile, a drink, a cold towel, my lawn chair and always a word of encouragement. Since they were available to take care of my needs and me, this allowed me the opportunity to focus on running. I was successful because of their efforts. Their willingness to give of themselves allowed me to stay the course. I will never forget their random acts of kindness. How can you go wrong by surrounding yourself with individuals like this? You can't! Now, you can see why my support team was such a source of strength to draw from.

Day after day I also drew upon my strength from the Lord. Therefore, the scripture verse found in Isaiah 40:31, holds a special place in my heart. I would remind myself of this great Old Testament promise. This verse was printed on our Sponsors banner that we proudly displayed in our many stops along Route 66. The verse says, *"But they that wait upon the Lord shall renew their strength; they shall mount up with wings as eagles; they shall run, and not be weary; and they shall walk, and not faint."* (Scripture quote from the King James Version of the Bible) This is one of my favorite promises in the Bible which I can hold on too.

We can eat all the nutritional supplements that meet the requirements for our bodies to perform at their full potential. In any exercise program you must have the proper diet. Sometimes we need the emotional, mental, or spiritual food to nourish our minds. So much strength is derived from within. When I was tired, I waited upon the strength that comes from God. I knew with this divine strength, I would not be weary and would not faint. Even with the blisters, the worn out knees, and the big dogs chasing me.

Attached to my computer screen in my office on a sticky note is a quote that reads, *"Enjoy the little things in life, for one day you may look back and realize they were the big things."* Reading that quote and absorbing its message serves as my moral compass for the day. It allows me to set priorities, focus on what is really important for that day, and encourages me to look for the "little things" that comes across my path. I've since found the lyrics to "Go the Distance" and one of the "little things" I do now is listen intently to the words. When I listen to the song it provides an opportunity for me to reminisce and start dreaming… again. Take a moment and read the following words that spoke to my heart, encouraged me and gave me the perseverance I needed to go the distance.

"I have often dreamed, of a far off place
Where a hero's welcome, would be waiting for me
Where the crowds, will cheer
When they see my face
And a voice keeps saying
This is where I'm meant to be

I'll be there someday
I can go the distance
I will find my way
If I can be strong
I know every mile

Will be worth my while
When I go the distance
I'll be right where I belong

Down an unknown road, To embrace my fate
Through that road may wander
It will lead me to you
And a thousand years, would be worth the wait

It might take a lifetime, but somehow I'll see it through
And I won't look back
I can go the distance
And I'll stay on track

No. I won't accept defeat
It's an uphill slope
But I won't lose hope

Till I go the distance
And my journey is complete

But to look beyond the glory is the hardest part
For a hero's strength is measured by his heart

Like a shooting star, I will go the distance
I will search the world, I will face its harms

I don't care how far
I can go the distance
Till I find my hero's welcome, waiting in your arms

I will search the world
I will face its harms

Till I find my hero's welcome
Waiting in your arms"

Written by David Zippel

I think you can see why this song became my theme song. I didn't know it at the time when running across the state, but these lyrics referred to everything I was about to do. The song refers to dreams, a voice that keeps saying, and an unknown road to embrace. The message in the song reminds you and me to stay on track, we won't accept defeat, and like a shooting star, I will go the distance.

What is your song? Do you have lyrics to a song that encourages you during the day? What quote, slogan or scripture verse do you hold on to that can serve as an exhorter for you? Let me encourage you to find one today! Write it on that "yellow sticky" note, and then write it within your heart. Find your "promise" today and hold on to it! Remember, *"Today's mighty oak is just yesterday's little acorn that held its ground."* So hold on, hold your ground and go the distance! Dreams do come true.

Chapter Nine

STATE LINE—END OF THE DREAM

The green rectangle Oklahoma mileage sign was a site to behold. It read, State Line 5 Miles. Of all the signs along Route 66, this was the one I was ready to see. For me, it's the end of a dream. Just five miles to go in reaching the Kansas state line and the finish line. It had been sixteen days since I left the Texas–Oklahoma border. In those two weeks my life had been changed forever. The miles I put my body through, the people I met along the way, the pain, and the tears of joy along with the big dogs would leave a lasting mark. Even today, just thinking about my journey across Route 66 brings back a multitude of emotions, mainly, joy and a sense of achievement. Whew! I did it! 397 miles are behind me. A mere 2,096,000 steps along the "Main Street of America." Now, I have miles of memories and life changing experiences all along the Mother Road.

I'm often asked the question, "What is your next dream?" So far, I haven't had any definite and vivid dreams. My friend Rudy Ruettiger says, "When you achieve one dream, dream another." In the Old Testament it says, "Where there is no vision, the people will perish." I do think about my next vision or dream. When will it appear and what will it say to me? I'm in no hurry to experience the dream, but I know that one is on its way. I just have to be available and sensitive to what comes my way.

My hope is that this book has encouraged you to live your dreams. I hope I have reminded you of the fact, that dreams still come true. I also hope that you will begin today to put a PLAN in place to live your dreams. Keep listening to your heart and mind and don't put off any longer the pursuing your dream. The world will be a better place because you took the time to prepare your mind, listen to your heart, act on it, and never give up on living your dream.

Remember the words of Eleanor Roosevelt who said, "the future belongs to those who believe in the beauty of their dreams." So, go now and experience your dreams.

In the move *Forrest Gump*, after running for three years, two months, fourteen days and sixteen hours, Forrest was asked, "Why did you run for such a long time. He replied, "I just felt like running." I think people were waiting from some profound statement of why he ran across America a couple times. Perhaps they wanted to hear some extraordinary reason for his running. He had no special reason, except for the fact he just felt like doing it. I hope after reading this book you will be like Forrest and just do it because you feel like it. Don't wait for all the stars to line up in sequence. Don't wait on the approval of others. Pursue your dream today because you just feel like it!

As I close my letter of encouragement to you, I would like to share with you a quote from Louise Driscoll. She once said, "*In your heart, keep one still, secret spot where dreams may go and sheltered so may and grow.*"

I wish you the very best, as you live your dreams!

*Dan Miyoshi and Bud Butler are posing next to a
Route 66 historical marker. I could not have made it
without the support of these two men.*

Lt. Governor Mary Fallin reading the Proclamation declaring Steve Kime Day in the State of Oklahoma.

Receiving an unforgettable hug from some
Helen Paul elementary students.

Running east down the Mother Road.
At this point, over halfway there!

THE DAILY
JOURNAL OF THE
DREAM

I kept a daily journal of my run, which has certainly helped me recall the numerous people, places and names. Sometimes, I was so exhausted that I didn't write in great detail but penciled in some quick notes about the day's activities. This will not be a play-by-play of those 16 days of running. I hope this portion of the book will speak to your heart and encourage you to keep moving down the highway to your dreams. I want to share with you some memorable stories, places visited, and individuals that filled up the pages and made my daily journal a keepsake for life.

At the end of each day, I was able to reflect back over the events during my day of running. Many of these events made a lasting impression. These impressions were what I called daily lessons of life. I learned a valuable lesson each day as I ran across the state. I want to share with you those lessons and perhaps they may be of help to you as you pursue your dreams.

MARCH 29, 2001

I t's 7:01am and I'm standing in the middle of Route 66 right smack on the Texas – Oklahoma border. I find a highway sign that says Texola. I know I am in the right place to start my run. It's a foggy cool March morning and the sun is just beginning to rise. I only managed about two hours of sleep the night before so I wasn't full of energy as I had hoped. Picture this! I'm standing alone on the straight and narrow two-lane highway, dense fog, haze of a sunrise, and a quiet peace in the air. It was like I was in a vacuum. I savored the quiet moment, said a prayer and then started running. The road heads west to Texas and east across Oklahoma. I'm heading east! No fanfare, no bands playing or send off crowd. A very tranquil beginning but appropriate for a man with a determination to run down this Mother Road all the way to Kansas.

Bud and Mary, my support team drop me off at the border and take off down Route 66 for about 5 miles. We will work as a team like this throughout the next sixteen days. I will run on the average five miles and catch up with the Winnebago and my new best friends. They will have a power bar, water, lawn chair, word of encouragement or whatever I need to keep running.

About two or three miles into the run I receive a call from Bud warning me of oncoming traffic. The fog was so dense in some places making it very difficult to see anything on Route 66. As I hung up my cell phone acknowledging Bud's warning, a pickup truck came roaring out of the fog. Near miss Number one! I'm thinking, maybe it's not such a good idea to run along Route 66 after all. Too late. I've committed to do it! I decided then to hug the shoulder of the road until the fog lifted. I encountered my first Route 66 dog, but he was a gentle friend. Little did I know that the mean dogs were way down the road waiting for their opportunity to meet me. This friendly dog ran with me for about one mile despite my encouragement for him to get home. I guess he served as my official send off partner and I enjoyed our brief one way conversation anyway.

Bud and Mary have made their way to Erick, Oklahoma. Erick would be our first official stop for us to meet with the townspeople and students. I catch up with the support team on the west edge of Erick and change into my Forrest Gump wardrobe. I meet with the Chief of Police and a minister of the First United Methodist Church of Erick after changing my clothes. They are excited about Forrest running through their city.

The kind minister says he will have a lighted candle in the church's Divine Mercy Prayer Chapel for the next sixteen days. I am moved with the caring compassionate spirit this man exhibits as he tells me the church will be praying for me each day on the run. I think now that maybe I can run this 397 miles.

Believe me, you want God on your side when you take on an event like this one. It is a good feeling for me to know that I will be on the minds and hearts of many people as I run each day.

Dressed in my plaid shirt, red cap, and khaki pants I'm ready to face the citizens of Erick, population about 1,000. I leave the support team and head for downtown. I can't believe the sight in front of me. I'm running down Route 66, directly through the middle of town and on both sides of the highway are students and residents holding these yellow smiley face "Have a Nice Day" signs and shouting the words, "Run Forrest Run!"

If you recall from the movie, Forrest was running across the country when a yellow t-shirt salesman came running along side and asked Forrest for some slogan advice. As the two men were running a truck splashed mud on Forrest's face and the t-shirt salesman handed him a shirt to wipe his face clean. Forrest handed the shirt back which left the muddy impression of a face on the shirt and said, "have a nice day." Thus the creation of the smiley face logo and slogan. All thanks to Forrest and of course Hollywood.

To my surprise hundreds of people have lined the streets to see Forrest. News releases were sent to all the cities that lined "America's Main Street" in Oklahoma, but I had no idea what the response would be. A flood of emotion overtook me. I was over-whelmed by the excitement and enthusiasm displayed by the people of Erick. I ran down the highway and did the standard "high-five" slapping of hands to as many people as possible. A few blocks later, the Erick high school basketball coach, my new Methodist minister friend, and the superintendent of schools joined me in my run through town. What a sight to behold! And what a sight that is imprinted in my memory for a lifetime.

My goal was to arrive at Sayre, Oklahoma by 5 pm. Thursday was a great day for a run weather wise. Temperature in the low 80's, clear blue Oklahoma sky, and not too much wind. From Erick to Sayre, I had the privilege of being escorted by an Oklahoma Highway Patrolman. I felt a little special to have this kind of pro-tection while running and mainly enjoyed the conversation with the Trooper as I made progress across Beckham county.

There wasn't much traffic for the day except for a few deer crossing the historic highway. Much of the original highway is left for viewing and not for driving. Many trees, bushes, and just good ole Oklahoma weeds have taken root through the payment. I ran on the original portion of Route 66 when possible, just so I could say I did. During the quiet moments of the run, the repetitious sound of my feet hitting the payment lured me into the state of reminiscing. When I would run on that old Portland cement surface, I would allow my mind to play the "I wonder game." It goes like this. I won-der if Pretty Boy Floyd drove down this stretch of the Mother Road. I wonder how many people stopped at this spot as they traveled to California. Did Elvis drive down this part of the pavement where I'm running? As you can imagine, the "I wonder game" can be fun, but mainly it gave me things to ponder about while running on the highway. Sometimes, it was so peaceful in those solitude moments that it was like the road was trying to share its secrets with me as I ran all alone. I have 397 miles ahead of me to listen to the Mother Road share its stories.

It is a rather uneventful run all the way to Sayre. My knees are starting to hurt so as I approach the western edge of the city I am relieved. I run downtown and am greeted by a reporter and photographer of the Sayre Record Newspaper. After a quick interview I am introduced to some Chamber of Commerce officials and then we receive great news. The news is about dinner. We are told that a special steak dinner is being prepared on our behalf. After 10 hours of running for the first day, I'm ready to do some serious eating. Mary, Bud and myself enjoy the best steak dinner and conversation with two of the finest people from Sayre. The steak is the size of a hubcap. It is huge! And the visit, gracious and memorable.

End of day one. Undoubtedly, one of the most memorable days I've ever experienced. With only two hours of sleep from the previous night, I'm ready to call it quits. No one will have to rock me to sleep tonight!

Lesson #1: Keep your head and heart going in the right direction and you will not have to worry about your feet. This is fun, living the dream!

Friday

MARCH 30, 2001

After breakfast at Deb's restaurant in Sayre, it's time to start running. My left knee still feels the mileage from Thursday's big day, but got to keep moving. I got places to go and people to meet.

It was a sunny, cool spring morning as I start out from the eastern edge of Sayre city limits. I was running on the Mother Road, which runs parallel with Interstate 40 in much of western Oklahoma. Actually, all the way from Sayre to Yukon, which is located just west of Oklahoma City, you can either see or heart the traffic that is traveling on I-40 while on Route 66.

I had been running for a couple of hours and as I am crossing one of the many bridges that exist on Route 66, a gentleman approaches in his pickup truck. Nothing new about me running into oncoming traffic. I've been doing this for two days now, but this time something seemed different. As the "cowboy" draws closer to me, he slows down his pickup and with his left hand throws a fist full of money in my direction. I stop, I look him straight in the eye, and he simply says, "this is for the Special Olympics athletes." He hits the gas pedal and takes off just as I say, "thank you." I later learn that he stopped along the side of the road when he passed the support team as they were waiting on me. As you recall, my support team would drive about five miles ahead of me and pull over to the side of the road and wait. This gracious gentleman stopped to see if they needed any assistance. Bud explained what we were doing, so when he passed me, he wanted to make his contribution to our cause, therefore he handed me a fistful of dollars.

I run a few more miles down the road and meet up with my support team. Bud tells me that during their wait on me, two different individuals pulled over to the side of the road and asked if they needed any help. I lost track of the numerous times that caring and compassionate Okie's pulled over to offer their assistance. Seriously, I believe that someone stopped if not once but twice each day during our sixteen-day journey across Oklahoma. I had forgotten about the kindness Sooners can offer.

The sunny weather from the morning hours continued on into the afternoon. Mother Nature cooperated this day. Not too much wind to run against which is rare in Oklahoma. I enjoyed the time on the road. It was a rather quiet day running. No dogs to outrun on this day. I had some rather long talks with myself as I ran down the Mother Road. It was one of those therapeutic runs. While exercising the body, I got the chance to exercise my mind as well!

We end the day just west of Clinton, Oklahoma.

> ***Lesson #2: When someone hands you cash money, or when someone offers their hand—take it! Seriously, I was moved by the generosity of this man and also of the many individuals that stopped and offered help. In a time when we are so busy going from point A to B, it was refreshing to know there are people that are willing to stop, go out of their way, and be of assistance. I am reminded that I need to slow down, take the time to help others, even if it means stopping or going out of my way.***

MARCH 31, 2001

Mother Nature decided to change her mind about the weather. It was very windy and humid day for a run. Not the weather I would order for a day of running, but that's Oklahoma. I stretch out all the muscles I can find and head out down the road. Bud and Mary take out in the Winnebago and will be waiting for me five miles down the road. After two days of traveling, we have become a great team. We are getting good at this. When I arrive at the Winnebago, Bud or Mary have my lawn chair, my energy bar and drink ready for me. They are troopers. They are enjoying this as much as me.

They will tell me quite often how much they like their role in this event compared to mine. Each day, I will ask and see if anyone wants to run with me. Mary and Bud assured me it was best they stayed with our "home on wheels."

My left knee is starting to hurt with a higher pain intensity. It has been hurting since the end of day one, but nothing this bad. I'm thinking I could be causing serious injury to my leg. I have to keep moving because we have a speaking engagement tonight. We have been asked to share our story to some young people and adults at a Methodist church in Weatherford later tonight.

Since the pain in the knee is rather excruciating, I start one of my pity parties. I feel that I'm in a predicament. I'm afraid I will not be able to continue my run. I'm concerned about all the people I will be letting down if I must stop. I begin second-guessing my abilities and motives about this run across Oklahoma. I'm beating myself up pretty good emotionally when I decide to make a phone call.

I place a call to my friend Dr. David Dyson. I've always been impressed by the wisdom David shares and exhibits in his own life. I explain my situation to him and he calmly replies, "Steve just remember, the objective is the same, but the strategy can change." As I discussed David's comment in the earlier portion of the book, I think it's important for us to remember we have options. That is one great thing about living in America. We have choices, options, and different avenues to take in life.

I feel this peace come over me as David shares his wisdom with me. I realize now, that I can get across the state and stay focused on the objective, but it may have a different strategy attached. I thank Dr. Dyson for his friendship, wisdom and words of encouragement and hang up the phone. I start race walking, which is a pace a little slower than jogging. I am Weatherford bound.

We get to the west edge of Weatherford and have to stop for the day. We must find a hotel where we can get a hot shower, warm-up from being in the cold wind, and get our thoughts together for our presentation at the church.

About fifteen young people and adults attend the social gathering at the church. Bud steps onto the stage, which is located in the front of the sanctuary and shares what this event means to him. I am impressed with the way he speaks from his heart. I speak for a few moments and share how all of this began as a dream. I end my talk by saying, "God has given me to ability to run, so why not do some good with my running." Mary is a little bashful, so she speaks from the church pew. She too speaks from the heart and shares her love for Special Olympics and why she gives of her time and talents to this organization.

We leave the church with $115 in donations to Special Olympics. We didn't ask for money, but the gracious congregation wanted to do their part to help Forrest run across the state. End of another memory making day.

Lesson #3: The objective is the same, but the strategy can change. I also learned the valuable lesson of having someone in your life that you can share your heart with. As you pursue your dream, it's important to always have someone 'in your corner" that will offer a word of encouragement and wisdom.

APRIL 1, 2001

The owner of the Mark Restaurant in Weatherford buys us breakfast. This is one thing that I'm enjoying about our trip across the Sooner State. We are eating well, and locating some of the greatest "ma and paw" restaurants along Route 66. We have plenty of food stored in the Winnebago for our daily journeys, but the three of us really look forward to finding a great place to have our evening meal or breakfast.

After a radio interview, it's time to hit the road running. This Sunday morning is cold, windy and the grayest clouds the Oklahoma sky has to offer. This is a good day to attend warm churches or simply stay inside the house. Not the best of running conditions. After living in Oklahoma for most of my life, you would think I would be used to the wind sweeping down the plains. Not so! This is suppose to be a spring day in April, but you wouldn't think so by just looking outside.

I'm heading east on Route 66 out of Weatherford, and you can hear the traffic sounds from nearby Interstate 40. Most of the noise is coming from the many eighteen-wheelers moving down the road. Today, the noise seems louder than it has been in the past. I realize the wind is howling from the south and seems to carry the highway noise my direction. Since most of my run today will be north of I-40, I will be hearing a lot of road noise today.

For the past few days, the traffic on I-40 served as entertainment.

At various points, Route 66 is just 100 yards north parallel to I-40. I can watch the traffic on the Interstate as I run. Watching the traffic gets my mind off the miles I run each day, and even helps with the pain in my knees. I play games with the truckers. As the big eighteen-wheeler trucks power their way down the Interstate, I make a pumping up and down motion with my right arm in an effort to get the truckers to sound their horns. I remember we would do this as kids when traveling with mom and dad on vacation. We would sit in the back seat of the car and when a truck would pass – we would start pumping our arms in hopes of getting a blast from the horn. Here I am, thirty five years later doing the same thing. Believe me, when running by yourself, you will find some kind of entertainment to get you through the day.

If anyone has ever driven down Route 66, they have heard about a place called Lucille's. It is a station that was established back in 1941. Today, it sits abandoned, but a sign swinging in the breeze let's you know that it is still Lucille's. Bud and Mary choose to park the Winnebago and use this historic landmark station as our resting spot. Landmark or not, I'm just glad they stopped so I could get out of the wind and rest.

As I'm running east of Hydro, a huge dog leaves the front porch of his farmhouse and is running as fast as his legs will take him. Problem is, he is running directly at me. The size of this dog increases as he gets closer. I realize that he doesn't want me running in front of his house. I'm thinking, "what did I ever do to you?"

I am so fortunate to find a hubcap on the side of the road and use it to defend myself. This dog is bad! Maybe he isn't used to people on his portion of Route 66? I look up and see the owner of this dog out in the yard. I can't believe it. This dog wants my leg or anything else he can get into his mouth and the man ignores my pleas for help. I keep running, swinging the hubcap at the dog and kicking at him when my stride permits. Finally, the dog gives up and goes back to the porch. Whew! Maybe this isn't such a good idea running across the state. I know that this mean dog is not related to my furry little friend that joined me on the first day of my run.

I keep running and my nerves settle back down. I continue moving eastward trying to get as many miles in as possible today. Since

I have been doing the walk, jog, running routine, I've been able to make good progress across the state without much aggravation to the knees. I'm thrilled that my knees are feeling better, but a new problem is just starting to surface. Blisters!

By the end of the afternoon I'm ready to call it quits. I'm tired of the dogs, the cold and the wind. As I keep running toward Bridgeport, I notice a young man, high school age out in a pasture feeding his horses. As I run by he waves and I decide to take a break and go over to the fence to visit. I discover his name is Peyton and every afternoon at this time he feeds his horses. I am impressed with the way the horses follow him. They were acting like pets, yet these huge and gorgeous brown and black horses look so powerful. I tell him I have been running along Route 66 for four days and explain to him why a grown man would do such a thing. Peyton seems rather impressed with this feat and promises to share with his family, his friends and teachers at school the next day of his encounter with a man dressed like Forrest Gump running across Oklahoma. I say goodbye, pet one of his horses and take off.

We end the day with a photo session at the historic Pony Bridge located west of Bridgeport. Since we are filming the run across the state, we try to include some of the historical places on Route 66 as the backdrop. The Pony Bridge is three quarters of a mile in length spanning the Canadian River and has 38 arches. The yellowish looking bridge was built in 1933 and is very narrow. We learn that it's just wide enough for a Winnebago to get across. In the movie *Forrest Gump*, it always seem to have a scene where Forrest was running across bridges. So, I thought it was perfect to use the Pony Bridge in our video documentary.

We find a motel in Hinton and rent some rooms. The three of us need some quiet time, a very hot shower, and rest. The end of another long day.

Lesson #4: You can't outrun the big dogs so keep a hubcap close by. Seriously, we will face various forms of weather as we pursue the dream. The wind will not always be at our back, and the sun may not always shine in our favor, but with a strong sense of direction and purpose, one will prevail.

APRIL 2, 2001

We start the day at the "Little Okie" restaurant in Hinton, Oklahoma that is located south of Route 66 on State Highway 281. Staying in the motel the previous night provided the rest we needed. We were re-charged and ready to go! Especially after eating pancakes, sausage, toast and all the coffee one could stand, I was ready to hit the road running.

As Bud and Mary are leaving the restaurant, I stay behind and apologetically interrupt a conversation between five local farmers. The scene is something you would see painted on a Norman Rockwell calendar. Small town eating establishment, old advertising signs hanging on the wall of the diner, and gathered around the breakfast table are several men focused on a discussion trying to solve the worlds problems.

I introduce myself to these men and ask them a question about a section of Route 66 that was taken up from the ground and transported to the Smithsonian in Washington, D.C. I had learned months earlier, that a section of the original Route 66 was being preserved and taken to the Smithsonian as part of an "Americana" exhibit.

One man at the table replied, "the section taken up is located east of Bridgeport. It's barricaded but you can still get close enough to see part of Route 66 is missing." I explained to them I was running across the state of Oklahoma, but they didn't seemed impressed at all. They didn't even question me why I would do such a thing.

They all just nodded in agreement that it was okay to run the length of Route 66. I thanked them for the information and hurried out the door to catch up with Mary and Bud.

I change clothes as we are driving back to the Pony Bridge near Bridgeport. We ended yesterday here at the bridge with a photo session. Today, it will be our starting point. Bud and Mary drive off to find the segment of Route 66 that has been removed, and I run to meet them. It isn't difficult to find the section of pavement that was removed, because the section had been filled in with black asphalt. You travel down Portland Cement base Route 66 and then all of a sudden it turns to black asphalt.

Portland Cement was used in thousands of miles all across the country in an effort to provide paved roads. Portland Cement is used chiefly to make concrete. This type of cement was named Portland because it has the same color as stone quarried on the Isle of Portland, a peninsula on the south coast of England.

I hope to go and visit the Smithsonian sometime soon and see the concrete section of Route 66.

Finding this segment of highway isn't as dramatic as hoped. But, it does create some excitement for us this morning. Now it's back to basics. Heading east on Route 66 and working our way toward El Reno. The weather is clear and the south wind is really kicking. The wind is blowing exceptionally hard today! We make our way down the Mother Road mile by mile. Our system is working rather well. Bud and Mary drive down the road a few miles and pull over and wait on me. We've been doing this for days now, and it is working in our favor. Thanks to my friend Randy Ellis, we have adopted the system Randy used in his run across the United States.

As we approach the western edge of El Reno, I notice highway signs on the side of Route 66 that said, *"Don't pick up hitchhikers. They may be prison escapees."* I don't think much about the message printed on the signs until I come within sight of the Federal Corrections Facility. This is the first time I've seen the facility, and I prefer being on the outside versus within. Some of the inmates are outside their buildings, but are kept inside by the coils of razor sharp wire that surround the prison. I receive a few glances and waves from the inmates as I run by and I hesitantly wave back.

I finally realize why some of the inmates are just standing in the prison yard and staring at me as I'm running down the road. It seems like a few of the inmates are mesmerized as I pass by the facility. About twenty yards behind me is an officer of the El Reno police department providing escort. The difference this time is that the officer is behind me to protect me from oncoming traffic.

I am tired and had forgotten about the officer behind me with patrol lights flashing. It looks like a scene out of Dragnet. Perhaps the inmates thought I was running from the law. At one of our rest stops, the officer and I joke about how it may have looked with me running and his following with the patrol lights flashing.

After about seven hours of running today, we decide to call it quits. I receive a call from Bud who finds a spot to park the Winnebago. Bud says to look off to the right and I'll find a City Park situated on Country Club drive. It takes me a few minutes to arrive but I spot the Winnebago. As I approach the park, I notice a group of boys playing baseball. I'm excited to reach the park, because I get to call it quits for the day. When I turn the corner I notice the young boys stop playing ball and come over to the side of the road and start cheering for me. Bud and Mary talked with them moments earlier and shared with the team my dream of running across the state. I run by the boys and their coaches, and "high five" each one to show my appreciation to them.

I am glad to stop after a long day of running into a wind that is "sweeping down the plains." I visit with the boys a few minutes and learn they are practicing for an upcoming game in their twelve year old baseball league. I feel impressed to share with them a story about surrounding yourself with the right kind of people. I challenge them to surround themselves with people that will encourage, enrich and enhance their life. Life is about making choices and we all want to make good choices. Choosing the right people to interact with is one key to a successful future.

We pose for a few pictures and exchange thank yous. The visit with the baseball team was a very encouraging ending for a long, hot, windy day of running.

My blisters are really causing problems and I need to take all the needed measures to prevent infection. They are bleeding significantly and I must take care of my feet. We covered a lot of miles today. It's time to rest and get off my feet. The end of the day is quickly becoming my favorite.

> *Lesson #5: Life's little opportunities to offer a word of encouragement come in many different ways. Whether it's showing up at a boy's baseball team practice, visiting with a next door neighbor, or crossing paths with a perfect stranger, God has a way of bringing people into our lives that need to hear a word of inspiration. Take a moment today and look for "life's opportunities" to encourage one another.*

Tuesday

APRIL 3, 2001

We begin this spring day like many others, eating. As I mentioned earlier in the book, I lost fifteen pounds during my 400 mile run while constantly eating. I did eat healthy and the right food groups along the way, but I was surprised at my appetite level during my run. I was always looking for my next meal! Another Denny's restaurant breakfast and we're set to go.

We begin the morning at the City Park located on Country Club drive. The twelve-year-old baseball team isn't there to see me off. Hopefully, these young men were in school since it was a school day. A member of the El Reno police department will be meeting us this morning at the park. This officer will be escorting me through downtown El Reno and east to the limits of the city. Also meeting us this morning before our run is a journalist from the El Reno Tribune newspaper. After a fifteen interview and a photo session with the reporter, it's time to start running.

I leave the park and head east toward downtown El Reno. Just like yesterday, I have a police escort and it's the same officer. His name is Tim and he is excited about being part of this run event across Oklahoma. Once again, he is following me in his patrol unit with lights flashing.

It is a few blocks into the run, when some local residents start shouting at me from across the road. As they shout at me, they are using their arms and hands and point behind me. It looks like they are trying to get me to look behind. Finally, one guy shouts from across the street, "look behind you buddy. There's a police officer trying to get your attention." I just laugh! I guess these folks have never seen anyone dressed like Forrest Gump running down Route 66 with a police escort. They thought I was being chased by a police officer. A little humor sure helps to get the morning run off to a good start. I wave back at them and say "it's okay. He's with me."

I reach the city-county line east of El Reno and it's time for the changing of the guard. I say good-bye to Tim, the El Reno officer that gave up an afternoon and morning to provide the escort through his fine city. Meeting law enforcement officers like this young man makes me proud. These are some of Oklahoma's finest putting their lives on the line for you and me. Tim had fun being part of our run and we felt privileged to have him participate.

At the county line a Canadian County Sheriffs Deputy meets me ready to meet the escort challenge of the day. He is there to provide protection and some companionship along the way to my next destination, which is Yukon.

This is turning out to be a really hot day. Not much wind to contend with today, compared to yesterday, but enough to provide a good wind burn on my skin. The exhaust fumes from the passing automobiles seem to linger on the roadway. As I'm running, the disgusting odor seems to be intertwined with the heat waves rising from the pavement. This is going to be another tough day running along the Main Street of America. Not much happens during my jog to Yukon. Just putting one foot in front of the other and waving to the motorist as they pass by.

I enter the city limits and once again am greeted by a law enforcement officer. This time it is a motorcycle officer from Yukon Police Department. This was going to be a little different experience because now I'm able to talk with someone as I'm running. It is a challenge to carry on a conversation with an officer behind the wheel of a patrol car. Now, I have someone right by my side. It helps to pass the time and the miles with my new escort buddy on my left. I run along the shoulder of Route 66 and he rides between me and the traffic.

As we enter downtown Yukon, I notice a young man standing on the curb about 50 yards in front of us with his arm extended away from his body. The closer I get to him, I notice he is holding something rather large in his hand. It is a water bottle. And not just any water bottle. It is a water bottle with the University of Oklahoma logo printed on the outside. How does this young man know that I was an OU grad? He doesn't! It is a hot day for a run and the reflection of the heat off the pavement makes things worse. This young man has compassion for me and stands at the street edge and hands me the bottle of water. I don't care what school logo is printed on the outside. His kind gesture is gladly accepted from this OU alum as I chug down the water.

Experiences like this one stand out in my mind as one of the highlights. When I recall events of my run across Oklahoma, I'm reminded of moments such as these. This is the first time during the past 150 miles that someone takes a moment out of their busy schedule and stands along side Route 66 to hand me some water. I am moved in my heart by this man's generosity and caring spirit. It is only bottled water, but he took the time to go in a store, pay for it, and then stand in the heat waiting for me to arrive.

Bud has pulled the Winnebago into a convenience store parking lot, and along with my motorcycle officer friend, I decide to take a break. I have put in around 18 miles for the day and with the heat, a rest sounds good. I never pass up a good chance to rest my knees and replace the bandages on my blisters.

We take a few minutes to cool down when two young girls come up to the Winnebago asking about Forrest Gump. Bud hands them two Special Olympic cards that are the size of a baseball card. We had hundreds of these cards printed to hand out to people we met as we traveled along Route 66. There is a picture of me dressed as Forrest with information regarding the purpose of my run printed on the backside. The girls asked me to autograph the cards and we pose for some pictures. This celebrity stuff is getting to be fun!

After a thirty-minute break, it's time to get moving. I must get to Bethany before dark. I race quickly into the convenience store and buy a water bottle. I wanted to remember this rest stop so I buy another OU bottle and place it inside the Winnebago. I have a place in the back of the motor home where I am storing all pieces of my run memorabilia. Posters, hubcaps, and business cards are among the few items in my collection.

It's about five o'clock in the afternoon and the heat is taking its toll on me. I have another five to ten miles to go to reach my final stopping point. When we leave the city of Yukon and enter the city limits of Bethany, once again it's time to say farewell to my new friend. Each time that I say good-bye and hello to the law enforcement officers, I hand them my journal and they have an opportunity to write a few words and then autograph a page for me. To "protect and serve" were motto's printed on many police cars I encountered during my 397 mile run. Each officer I met did a great job in carrying out that promise. I will always be grateful to them.

I'm still running east along the Mother Road. I have been heading this direction for the past eight hours. Bud and Mary have gone up ahead in the Winnebago waiting for me to catch up. On the western edge of Bethany, there is an old bridge on Route 66 that spans the North Canadian River. It isn't open for much traffic these days, but it's an opportunity for Bud to do more video recording. Many of these old bridges found on the Main Street of America still stand proudly to this day. They were designed to span a river and to keep traffic moving. These magnificent steel structures like many of the others I ran across are very narrow and provide a special excitement for me as I run. I love history and as I run across the bridge I hope it will whisper to me some of its secrets. Imagine the different people that traveled across this steel and concrete span. Did Elvis cross this bridge? How many people going to California crossed the bridge, got out of their cars, and took a brief swim in the river? There is a certain mystique surrounding these old structures that decorate the Mother Road.

We end a very hot and long day of running at Bethany. We covered a lot of miles today, and made many new friends. This was a fun day for everyone involved in the run across Canadian County.

Lesson #6: Life is a series of choices. Choices to do good or to do bad. A choice to offer kindness or to offer nothing. This young man made a conscious choice to help and to offer assistance to me a perfect stranger. How many people do you know are willing to take a moment out of their day to help another. I will always remember his kind deed, and his outstretched hand, which reminds me that I too should make the choice to help a perfect stranger.

APRIL 4, 2001

Wednesday is the day we say good-bye to Mary. Besides a wonderful wife to Bud, I found Mary to be a gracious and kind woman. She has given her time and limitless energy to be a part of the support team. She always seemed to know when I needed that power-bar! Mary has a big heart and has given much during her time with us on the Mother Road. I learned a few more things about Mary during the trip. For years she has volunteered countless hours and provided loving hugs to many Special Olympic athletes in Oklahoma.

When Mary and Bud agreed to be my support team, they had to make some adjustments at home. They had to make sure someone would take care of their dogs. With names like Samson and Titan, you better make sure you find the right person to accommodate the needs of these Rottweilers. I know it was difficult for both of them to be away from their children. This unselfish act tells you a lot about Bud and Mary. My friend Mary will be missed.

Wednesday also turns out to be a short day of running. I sleep in and get some much needed rest for the blisters and knees. Bud and I take our time at a Denny's restaurant and graze on breakfast foods. Breakfast time is good for our stomachs and allows us the opportunity to chart our course for each day. Many a decision to solve the world's problems is made over a cup of coffee. Our destination today is the state capital, so we don't have very far to go.

We leave the city of Bethany and run east to May Avenue. As we approach the Oklahoma City metro area, I notice a substantial increase in traffic along Route 66. I am grateful for the police protection and escorts that we were receive as we move forward to the Capital.

Within the city limits of Bethany, Route 66 becomes a very busy highway. Route 66 now becomes a four-lane highway with heavy traffic. As we leave Bethany I don't have the escort protection as in the past. Bud is driving the Winnebago and following me as I make my way to May Avenue. I feel rather safe with a large motor home blocking traffic. Since I'm "allergic" to car bumpers, I appreciate Bud's willingness to run interference for me while I run. As I approach May Avenue, I make a turn south to 23rd street. If you follow the original maps of Route 66, this is the way to go. There are alternate routes of the Mother Road, but we wanted to run and experience as much of the original road as possible.

We are met at 23rd and May Avenue by two members of the State Capital Patrol. Bud had once again called ahead and let the police officials know of our whereabouts. They gave me instructions to stay on 23rd and head east. They will be following me, and keeping cars off my backside. Just like Route 66 in Bethany, 23rd street is a busy place. Many people pass by in their cars and shout, "Run Forrest Run." Many drive by and shout a few obscenities. I find it so amazing how people behind the wheel of the car view my running efforts. There are numerous people that would drive right next to me and talk to me as I run. They want to know what I am doing, what is the cause, and how far I have to go. There are also people that drive right along side of me and tell me that I am holding up traffic and a real nuisance to them. However, most Sooners behind the wheel are gracious and kind!

I'm heading east to the State Capital and Bud drives on ahead to meet me in the parking lot. This is a very humid day and not the day for a long run. Once again, I'm glad this will be just a short jog to the Capital. Humidity, heavy traffic, enough exhaust fumes for everyone, makes me wonder why I'm doing this running today.

I arrive late in the morning at the Capital. Bud is there with video camera in hand. I am attracting a lot of attention since I'm slowing down traffic and have the Capital Patrol escort with their lights flashing. After two hundred miles you would think I am accustomed to the attention. Not so, when you're running on pavement designed for automobiles you never get too relaxed and comfortable. I am still very "allergic" to car bumpers!

I catch my breath and take a few photographs with my two new friends. These gentlemen from the Capital Patrol are very gracious with their time and escort efforts. They sign my journal book and wish me well.

I didn't know then, but they would see me again the next day. These two officers inform me they would be there Thursday morning to provide an escort for me as I depart the State Capital complex.

Bud and I check into a hotel on north Lincoln Boulevard for an afternoon of rest. I had to get more ice on my knees and my blisters are bleeding badly. I take the afternoon off to let my body re-group.

Since we are constantly looking for our next meal, Bud makes a few phone calls and took me to Sleepy Hollow for a steak dinner. The owner of the restaurant is generous and provides two free steak meals and all the trimmings. We do a serious job of eating this evening. I don't feel any pain with my knees or blisters after eating all of that delicious food. One of the waitresses is fascinated by my running effort. She thinks my run is a noble cause. Somehow, we get on the subject of Jim Thorpe. The waitress had recently visited Jim Thorpe, Pennsylvania and I share with her that Jim Thorpe was my second-cousin. Bud and I have a great visit with everyone at the restaurant and gain about ten pounds after all the great food.

Another photo session with our new friends and we're off. This time we are headed to Will Rogers World Airport. My friend Dan Miyoshi is flying in to Oklahoma City tonight. We want to be on hand to give Dan a memorable Oklahoma welcome!

Lesson #7: It's important to follow your dreams even if others do not believe in you! Not everyone may view things the same way. The vast majority of people I met during my sixteen day run were very supportive and accommodating. A few individuals did not share the same enthusiasm. I learned today, not everyone will agree with my dream or desires and goals. I recall the old English proverb that says, "Keep company with those that may make you better."

APRIL 5, 2001

This spring day will be a day of big surprises. I am looking forward to this day, because in a ceremony on the steps of our State Capitol, there is going to be a declaration of designating April 5th as Special Olympics Day in Oklahoma. I am so proud and thrilled that my Special Olympic friends will be receiving such special notoriety.

One of my friends Teresa Sneed, a parent of a Special Olympian provides this story.

"We were standing on the south steps of the Oklahoma Sate Capital. My daughter, Nikki Sneed, had been asked to intro-duce Lt. Governor Mary Fallin. Her fellow athlete, Chris Paynter was to introduce Captain Philip Carr of the Oklahoma City Police Department. Nikki and Chris are Special Olympic Oklahoma athletes who had just returned from representing Oklahoma in the World Winter Games in Anchorage, Alaska. Also speaking that day was Bill Wiggins, Chairman of the Board of Directors for Special Olympics Oklahoma and Susie King of Conoco. There was a large crowd gathered, many from Conoco, Cingular Wireless and Dollar Rent A Car. Suddenly, we spotted someone running towards the Capitol and he just kept coming and ran right up the steps of the Capitol. It was Forrest Gump! Well, actually

it was Steve Kime. He had stopped by the Capitol during his run across the state. Of course, Forrest had a few words to say to the crowd before he continued his run."

It is a few minutes passed noon and the ceremony is well underway. A few presentations are made and then the introduction of Lt. Governor Mary Fallin. The Lt. Governor makes a few remarks and then catches me off guard. She calls me over to the podium and starts to read this document. I am thinking that she is reading the proclamation that declares this day to be Special Olympics Day in Oklahoma. As Lt. Governor Fallin reads the document, she gets to a line that reads,

"Now Therefore, I, Frank Keating, Governor of the State of Oklahoma, do hereby proclaim April 5, 2001, as STEVE KIME DAY in the State of Oklahoma."

As she is reading this statement, I think, whoa, wait a minute, there's a mistake here. This is suppose to be a proclamation for Special Olympics." I later learn that the Oklahoma Special Olympic staff in Tulsa decided to make it a STEVE day and have their declaration later on in the year during the Summer Games which are held in Stillwater. I am thrilled, overwhelmed and moved to tears. What a big surprise! My Special Olympics friends did a great job in keeping a secret.

The Lt. Governor places in my hand the Declaration and invites me to address the crowd. As soon as I begin to speak, the microphone goes silent. Do you remember the time in the movie when Forrest, dressed in his military uniform, proudly displaying his Medal of Honor, when he addressed thousands of people at the Lincoln Memorial and Mall pond?

As Forrest begins to speak, the microphone goes silent. He is standing there at the podium speaking to thousands, but they are unable to hear him. The microphone doesn't work. Picture this, I'm standing behind a podium which is centered on the south steps of the State Capitol, addressing those that gathered for the Proclamation, and no one can hear me because the microphone doesn't work. The wind is blowing so my voice isn't traveling at all towards the audience.

Jokingly, I refer to this particular scene and feel it is appropriate that this special day would follow just like it was portrayed in the Forrest Gump movie. The audience laughs because many of them distinctly recall the scene in the movie that I'm referring too. I shout a few words of gratitude. A word of thanks to those in attendance, to the Special Olympics athletes, and to God for giving me the health and ability to run across the state.

I walk away from the podium in a slight daze. I can't believe that this old boy from Perry, Oklahoma is honored with a day. Later, the Lt. Governor told me I should be very proud of this proclamation. She went on to say, "Many times individuals that have a day proclaimed in their honor are usually dead and gone."

This day I am very much alive because I can still feel the pain from the blisters and my knees. What an honor and surprise that I will always cherish.

After interviews with various news media that are represented, it is time to run. Often this is a most difficult time for me. It's so much fun visiting with new friends, and time to get backing to running on Route 66.

When you spend so much time alone running, you really look forward to the moments of visiting and sharing experiences with people you meet. I must admit I'm full of energy and adrenaline. I'm pumped! After the meeting at the Capitol, I'm ready to hit the Main Street of America one more time.

I say my good-byes and start running north on Lincoln Boulevard also known as Route 66. I'm escorted down the street by the State Capitol police and by the Oklahoma City Police Department. Here I am, running down the street dressed in khaki pants, blue checkered shirt and my red Bubba Gump shrimp hat. I really do look like Tom Hanks, according to many Sooners that witnes my running. I'm near the curb running north with the escorts behind me when all of a sudden a black woman called out my name. She said, *"Forrest, Forrest Gump! I'm so glad to meet you."* She hugged me like I was her long lost son. That woman can hug!

She asked, "what are you running for?" She keeps asking me

questions on why I'm running, and I flash back to the scene in the movie where television crews surround Forrest and reporters asking him why he was running.

To tell you the truth, this woman scared me. In my first 175 miles of running along Route 66, this was my first major hug! I was caught off guard in a big way! When she ran out in the street to hug me, I wasn't sure if I was being mugged or hugged! I quickly explained to her why I was running and I told her, I must keep moving. She blew a kiss at me and I waved back in return as I get back to running. That meeting with the jovial woman was quick, scary, but fun! You know ... she provided the only hug I got as I ran 397 miles across the state.

I'm running away from Oklahoma City and enter the city limits of Edmond. I'm escorted once again by America's finest policeman. This Thursday turns out to be a rather warm day. Temperatures reach into the upper 80's. I am really feeling the heat and the miles when I reach the east side of Edmond. I run to the intersection of Route 66 and Interstate 35. I-35 runs north and south dividing Oklahoma while the Mother Road runs west to east.

My mind, feet, and knees are ready to call it quits. This was a good day! A few surprises don't hurt anyone. From the Declaration at the Capitol, to the hug from the woman on the street, this was definitely a "red letter" day. My daughter was able to attend the ceremonies at the Capital and had these thoughts regarding the run across the state.

"When I first found out that my dad wanted to run as "Forrest Gump" across Oklahoma, my first thought was "you have got to be crazy, how embarrassing." When I realized what it was for, I was so proud. When he told me that he was running Route 66 and asked me to run with him, I thought he was insane.

I would get to hear his experiences every day, while he was on the road. He would call to tell me what animals he talked too, or the people who ran with him, or conversations he had with the animals, mainly cows and dogs.

One of the most special days for me was when "Forrest"

ran to the Capitol. It was a chance for me to meet some of the Special Olympic athletes. Their faces lit up when they met dad. At that moment, I knew my dad was helping these athletes accomplish their goals or help make their dreams come true.

Not many people can say "my dad ran across Route 66 in Oklahoma."

Lesson #8: When you can, do something to make your "momma" proud! What a thrill, surprise and honor to receive a Proclamation Day in my honor. I hope to be able to give back to Oklahoma and Special Olympics and be worthy of this honor. I am reminded of this quote by Pierre Charron. "He who receives a benefit should never forget it; he who bestows should never remember it."

Friday

APRIL 6, 2001

Arcadia to Chandler. A windy, sunny day greets Dan, Bud and myself as we continue eastward. Today, we begin in the center part of the state. We begin our trek along the "Main Street of America" by crossing Interstate 35, which runs north and south through the entire state. Our final destination today is Chandler. Tonight, we are scheduled to meet with the Chandler City officials and have dinner where a presentation to honor Special Olympics will be given. Got to keep moving!

I'm having a little difficulty getting started this morning. Bud and my new support team member Dan are ready to go, but my body is saying no! Yesterday, with all the festivities and media attention at the State Capital in Oklahoma City and Edmond, there is a little emotional let down because all the fanfare is over and all there is left to do now is run!

We make our way to Arcadia, site of the historic "Round Barn," which was built back in 1898. The barn is listed on the National Register of Historic Places. The barn is positioned just to the north of Route 66 and it's a sight you don't want to miss. Sitting just a few yards off the highway, the barn is very large, very round and thanks to a recent paint job very red. With these characteristics, it's worth your time to take a few minutes to tour the historic "Round Barn."

After a photo session to document our visit, we move on to our next stop Luther. I have driven this portion of Route 66 from

Chandler to I-35 numerous times. It is one of the busiest sections of the road. I have dodged cars and trucks for the past eight days, but I know this stretch of "66" is going to be a little scary. Thanks to the Oklahoma County Sheriff's office and the Lincoln County Sheriff's Department, I am protected. I remember the Lincoln County cars had the words "to protect and serve" printed on the patrol car doors.

They certainly live up to their mission. My escorts follow me, giving me a sense of safety. I thought, "if I am going to be hit from behind, they have to go through a patrol car first!"

I am really looking forward to arriving at Luther because my father lives there. We are making great progress despite the strong south wind, the hills, and the heavy traffic. Bud and Dan, my support team, arrive ahead of me at Luther and locate my dad sitting in his pickup truck off to the side of the road. Dan gives me a call on my cell phone to let me know that everyone is waiting for my arrival. I'm running as fast as my blistered feet and hurting knees will allow me. When I come over the hill, it is exciting to see everyone in the distance waiting for me. Little did I know that, at this stage in my life, I would have this unique opportunity to have a "sit down" reminiscing visit with my dad along the Mother Road.

Dad and his wife Sue are waiting at the intersection of Route 66 and Luther exit. They seem glad to see me, but shake their heads in disbelief as they visit with a young man dressed in a plaid blue shirt, khaki pants, and a red "Bubba Gump" baseball cap. I haven't seen my dad in several months and here we are on the side of "Main Street of America" having a conversation.

We decide to sit on the tailgate of his new Chevy pickup truck (kind of an Oklahoma thing to do) and I share with him the events of the last eight days of running along the Mother Road. Of course, I have to show him the "notorious" blisters on my feet. He also tells me that a newspaper from Midwest City had interviewed him and asked for his reaction to my run across the state. My dad said he felt like a celebrity being interviewed by all the newspaper reporters. It makes me feel good to hear about the special attention he is receiving because of the run. He is a rather reserved man and is often heard saying, *"If you think it's bad now, wait' til later."* Not the kind of encouraging words I needed to hear at this stage of the run. After a forty-five minute rest and visit, it is time to get chugging on to Chandler. That's exactly how I feel, like a train just barely chugging along. We said our good-byes and I take off running again through Lincoln County headed towards Wellston and then to Chandler.

It was months later when my dad C.L. Kime shared his thoughts with me regarding our special day together on Route 66.

"I didn't see how you could do it. I was so excited to see your support team van arrive on the outskirts of Luther and meet Bud and Dan. These guys are characters for sure. I was thinking, how could you do it? How could you still be standing after running after all those miles? I thought, it sure takes a lot of courage to do this. I was so proud of what you were doing for the Special Olympic athletes. I also felt sorry for you because I knew you were tired and weary, but knew you could do it. You arrived at Luther with an intense look of exhaustion and determination on your face.

I realized that what you were doing took a lot of strength and determination. I also realized that if you set your mind to it, regardless of what the task is, and determine in your heart to do it, you're going to die trying. I remember when a stranger came up to me on day and said, 'hey did you hear about this Kime's kid who is running across the State? I said, "yes, that was my son." Just made me real proud to know you were helping Special Olympics and that the whole state knew it.

I have driven to Chandler from Luther numerous times. I thought it was impossible for anyone to run to Chandler. But, you took off running eastward down Route 66 towards Chandler just like it was done every day. I'm gonna remember this feat for a long time.

I arrive on the outskirts of Chandler about 6:00 p.m. Waiting on my arrival is Jamie Jenkins of the Lincoln County Newspaper. After a brief interview, we are introduced to Lt. Todd Carpenter and Officer Larry Thornton of the Chandler Police Department. After the introductions, I am told I need to run one more mile to a point where the presentation is to be made.

I ams running along Route 66 through downtown Chandler and stop on the edge of downtown at an old Phillips 66 Service Station. It is the old "cottage" style station. I worked for Phillips Petroleum back in the 1980s so I recognize the early day gas station building. On behalf of the residents of Chandler, Lt. Carpenter presents me a large white jug container containing cash and coins. The jug contains approximately $700. The generous people of Chandler conducted a fund-raising effort on behalf of Special Olympics the previous weeks and the Lieutenant presented the gift to me.

This is what it's all about. A chance for individuals within a community to give of themselves. This is a memorable and rewarding finish to a long day on the road. After a pizza dinner, it is off to the hotel for a warm shower and plenty of ice to pack around my knees.

> **Lesson #9: Do whatever you can to build and nurture your support system. With the support of family and friends, how can anyone not achieve their dreams?**

APRIL 7, 2001

My new friends Lt. Carpenter and Officer Thornton are escorting me today. Officer Thornton had a special interest in his escorting efforts today because his daughter was running alongside me.

It is an unusually cold Saturday April morning as Jessica and myself start our run through Chandler on Route 66. A cold front has moved through the area the night before and brought a typical Oklahoma thunderstorm with high winds, hail, and heavy ran. There is a smell of freshness in the cold air, as a result of the previous night's storm.

The following story was written by Officer Larry Thornton:

"As they started running that morning, I couldn't help but feel pride. My daughter had made a choice... and I believe it was the right choice.

Several weeks earlier, as the preparations were made for Steve Kime's historic run through Chandler, I had tried to arrange for the local track teams to join Steve as he ran through Chandler. Unfortunately, what I hadn't counted on was that a track meet would remove that possibility for both the varsity and junior varsity teams, leaving only the sixth-grade team, which included my daughter Jessica.

On Friday evening Steve's arrival went pretty much as

planned. There could have been more people lining the street, but the citizens of Chandler had already opened their hearts and their pocketbooks for the Special Olympics fundraiser and the local media was ready and waiting to document the arrival of "Forrest Gump," as portrayed by Steve.

But then problems began to arise. Although we knew our daughter's band was scheduled to play Saturday morning, and knew that several track team members were in band, we didn't realize how many that entailed. And while we'd made arrangements with the sixth-grade coach to ask his team to participate in the run the next morning we weren't sure whom or how many actually planned to be there. So when Steve asked if it might be possible to bump the starting time up an hour, allowing him to get more running in during a cooler part of the day, it's not surprising that our frantic attempts to reach the coach and some of the track team members were unsuccessful.

I still remember my darling daughter asking me that Friday night what she should do if the other team members didn't show up the next morning. I didn't tell her that she had to run, but I did point out that the track team members who did participate would be representing both the community and the police department in a very important event. With that in mind, Jessica made the decision to run the next morning no matter if she were surrounded by her teammates or alone at "Forrest's" side.

The next morning was cool, but thankfully not cold as Jessica and Steve stretched out a bit, no doubt wondering if anyone else would show up at the last minute. No one else came. At one point Steve looked over at my son, Jessica's younger brother, and asked if he would like to run as well. It was no surprise when he declined. By the designated starting time it was clear that the police department would only be escorting two runners through town.

With one police unit in the lead with red and blue lights flashing and my unit bringing up the tail, we took Steve and Jessica down the eastbound lane of Rt. 66. As they ran, I couldn't help but think "woe to anyone who crossed that cen-

terline between our patrol units, endangering the runners." I mean Steve's a great guy—like Will Rogers his enemies are definitely in the minority—but Jessica is my firstborn. However, I also felt something else... as I said earlier, I felt pride.

Steve's long stride, worn down by the miles and miles he'd already traveled, his swollen knees, tortured by their repeated impact with the pavement, was still longer than that of my little sixth grader, but she ran easily, her short pony tail bobbing steadily... a lasting memory of mine.

This day was one of the proudest days of my life, surpassed only by Jessica's birth and the day she accepted Christ Jesus as her Lord and Savior. Jessica had made a decision not to follow the pack... not to turn away when her teammates' decision not to participate focused more of the spotlight on her. Jessica doesn't compete in the Special Olympics, but she made a decision to participate in it. It was an individual effort on her part, but when she ran she carried the hearts of her community with her, including mine.

One of the reasons the Special Olympics is a worthwhile event is because it celebrates individual achievement. No matter how much support a participant receives from friends and family... no matter how much encouragement and love that participant receives from the sideline... part of what makes the event special is that the participant must reach down inside him or herself and search for that inner drive that says "I'm a somebody... I'm not part of the pack. I may not be the first over the finish line, but I'm going to win the race. ...I won it when I left the starting block."

After another photo session at the edge of town, it is once again the time to say good-bye and share our thank you's to the many gracious people in the town of Chandler. Stroud America is my next stop!

We make it to the western edge of Stroud and we decide to rest in the parking lot of a Phillips 66 station. I'm inside the Winnebago with ice packed around my knees. I'm drinking my powerade while taking a break before we meet up with the Mayor and some Special Olympic athletes from Stroud. Bud and Dan are outside the

Winnebago talking with some bikers. I learn that these five bikers are on their way to visit the Oklahoma City Memorial. It is a gorgeous day and who wouldn't want to be on their bikes out for a spring ride along Route 66.

I have no idea what Bud and Dan are visiting with them about, but a young man named Shaun comes to the door of the Winnebago and knocks politely on the side of the motorhome. Shaun introduces himself and hands me fifty dollars in cash money. He says he and his four friends admire my efforts for running across the state and he appreciates my willingness to help Special Olympic athletes and wants to help. I tell him, I appreciate his cash donation and willingness to help these athletes with his contribution.

I remove the ice packs that surround my knees and step out onto the parking lot to thank the other bikers. I thank and shake the hands of each biker. I have five more new friends and I've only been in the city of Stroud for a few minutes. We pose for a few pictures and as our new biker friends put on their helmets, I put on a smile of gratitude for their generosity. This is just another impromptu moment in my run across Oklahoma.

We must get moving because the City Officials and some athletes are waiting for us at Centennial Park. I'm running down Route 66 that runs directly through downtown Stroud. I look to my left and right and admire once again the architecture of some very old brick buildings. Bud and Dan go ahead and wait for me at the Park. As I'm running, I am joined by two young boys on their bicycles. I have a police escort behind me, so the boys are excited to be in this one man parade. There is a crowd of about eight people waiting on my arrival.

I am greeted by the Stroud Chamber of Commerce President and the Mayor. Two Special Olympic athletes and their families also greet me. I am presented with a check for $475 dollars to be used for Special Olympic programs. What a surprise for me! I am thrilled to receive the money, but pleasantly surprised by the generosity of these fine people of Stroud. We talk a few minutes about my experiences of running across Oklahoma and pose once again for some photographs. The local newspaper reporter is present and takes a few more pictures of the festivities. These events are what I look forward too. The chance to meet individuals from all walks of life,

Steve Kime

that have a common interest to make the difference in the life of a Special Olympic athlete. I can't wait to get the film developed so I can re-live these moments.

The Mayor of Stroud informs me that lunch is being bought for the three of us. I'm not that hungry, but Bud, Dan and myself haven't turned down a meal yet. We are accustomed to saying good-bye to our new friends. We just get to know our new friends and then it's time to say farewell.

We leave Centennial Park and walk to the infamous Rock Café. This café has been on Route 66 since day one. The building was built with rock unearthed during the paving of Route 66. The rock is brown in color and from a distance the outside walls of the building resembles a mosaic of various brown shades of rock.

The three of us enjoy a hamburger lunch compliments of the owner. I have my first bottle of Route Beer 66. The "root beer" drink comes in a dark brown glass bottle and has a white colored logo in the shape of a Route 66 highway sign. It was good root beer, but I bought the bottle mainly for my "collection" of paraphernalia I've acquired during my run.

Bud is able to round up ten dollars in additional contributions before we leave the Rock Cafe. We step outside and take a few pictures with the owners to document the event. We thank our generous friends for lunch and the donation and head off down the road.

I'm not running too fast this time, since my hamburger is freshly positioned on my stomach.

More running and more video taping of my journey down the historic Main Street of America. Sapulpa is our next destination.

Lesson #10: As we hurry down life's highway, take a few moments to help another along the way. The gracious bikers taught me something new about giving.

Even though they were on a "mission" to get to Oklahoma City, they took the time to help us with the cause.

APRIL 8, 2001

There were a few impromptu events during my run across Oklahoma. These unexpected events brought a great deal of excitement to the team. One event was the cowboy handing me cash money as he passed by me in his pickup truck. Another such moment was when a young boy joined me for a run down main street in Sapulpa. Dan, Bud and myself had arrived in Sapulpa early that afternoon. Route 66 goes right through downtown. I enjoy running through the many of the towns on the Mother Road because many of the early 1900's buildings are still standing. I love history, so when I get a chance to see a building that was erected in 1907, this is fun and exciting for this history buff. Downtown Sapulpa is a city with many old buildings that line main street and stand proud today.

As I'm running through downtown, I notice a little boy about ten years of age sitting on a park bench. I think he is practicing to be a Forrest Gump. As you recall, in the movie, Forrest was always sitting on a park bench discussing his life experiences to whoever would listen. I stopped to rest a moment and visit with him briefly. He asks me, "Is it alright that I run with you?" He is dressed for the occasion, as he is wearing a soccer uniform. I said, "come along. Let's go." So, we run just a block together down Route 66. Bud is videotaping our run together, so this young boy is excited about being in the movies. I run back with him to the park bench to make sure he is safe and is back where he belonged.

I didn't catch his name, but for a few minutes, my new friend provided some needed companionship as we ran together. It's a pleasant memory on the tape that shows the two of us running down main street Sapulpa.

Channel 6, a local television station from Tulsa has been tracking my run since I left Oklahoma City. I received a couple calls throughout the day today inquiring about my arrival in Tulsa. All I know is that it will be late in the day. Channel 6 wants to air the story on their Sunday night newscast, so they were anxious to film me while running. They decide to meet me in Sapulpa and do the interview.

I remember talking with their news director and he asked, "how will we find you?" I said, "I'll be the only guy dressed like Forrest Gump and running along Route 66." He laughed, realizing it will not be difficult to spot a Forrest look-a-like running along the Mother Road.

On the northeast edge of Sapulpa, we meet up with the Channel 6 news crew. We take a needed rest to conduct the interview and the cameraman does his thing by taking a video of my running. I have a little more strength in my step, because I'm running to Tulsa. I'm running to my home! I'm looking forward to spending the night in my bed.

I arrive in Tulsa late Sunday afternoon. I run across the 11th Street bridge and call it quits. The 11th street bridge is officially closed to traffic, but that doesn't stop me from running about a quarter of a mile across the Arkansas River. Like many of the old abandoned sections of Route 66, you just have to run, touch and experience the original sections of the Mother Road.

This is familiar territory for me. I've been running the River Parks pathway for years. Riverside Drive and 11th street has been a turn around point in my run for ages. There's a water fountain at the end of the jogging path. This is a good point to drink up, rest, and return to the starting point.

Today's ending was a little different than in the past days. This time, I'm leading the way. Instead of me running to catch up with my support team, I'm letting them follow me to the stopping point of my choice. Once we arrive at 11th street, we say good-bye to our

Oklahoma Highway Patrol escort that joined us between Sapulpa and Tulsa. I get in the Winnebago with Bud and Dan, our new destination is my home.

> *Lesson #11: It is a great education and incredible experience to see things during our travels. I think it is important for individuals to travel and see how the world lives. There is something comforting about coming home. A safe place that you call your own. There's no place like home. You're right Dorothy, there's no place like home.*

APRIL 9, 2001

We begin a sunny, warm Monday morning right where we left off from Sunday afternoon. Starting point today is 11th and Riverside.

Bud, Dan and myself are met by a huge escort team. The Tulsa Police Department sent three cruisers and about a half-dozen motorcycle officers. Now, this is an escort! I introduce myself to the Sargent in charge of Special Events. I share with him and the other officers a brief rundown of the past eleven days or running. They were pleased to be part of this statewide event and were ready to lead the way to Tracy Park. Tracy Park is located on Route 66 near the intersection of 66 and Peoria. Today, it will be Special Olympics Day in Tulsa. This city park is the designated location for the festivities starting at 12 noon.

Joining me in the run from 11th and Riverside to Tracy Park are three of my Tulsa friends. Suzanne Wallis, Mike Ponder and John Swasho.

Mike made the mistake one day of quipping, "if you are running across the state then I will run with you in Tulsa." Mike is a healthy individual but not a runner. I admired Mike for keeping his word.

Suzanne is running with me because she wants to support me and be a part of this event. She has seen Route 66 numerous times, but not necessarily on foot.

My Comanche Indian friend, John Swasho, has a Native

American name "Poyanee" which means "Always Walking." Well, today, John is "always running" with me along Route 66.

The four of us stretch our leg muscles and line up behind the motorcade. We are ready to go. Channel 8, a Tulsa television station is present to film our departure. I'm excited to see all of this attention with regard to my run. It makes up for all those lonely miles that I ran with no one around. With the motorcycles in front and police car units behind us we are escorted along 11th street, the official Route 66 in the city limits of Tulsa.

It doesn't take us long to reach Tracy Park and the one hundred plus people participating in the Special Olympic celebration are waiting.

The festivities at Tracy Park center on recognizing Special Olympics and the athletes. City Councilman, Special Olympic Executives, Tulsa Police Department officials, and Corporate Sponsors are given their moment behind the microphone to share their thoughts. It is a proud time for me to witness the celebration and share some of the recognition my run across the Sooner State is generating.

One of the toughest things for me emotionally is the continuation of running after events like these. When you are surrounded by many individuals and have the chance to visit with others, sometimes it is difficult to say good-bye and move on. Since I spend the majority of the time running in solitude, I look forward to mingling with others. A few more interviews with different television stations and once again, it is time to say good-bye. It is difficult this time, because I am saying so long to many new friends. Even more so, I am saying good-bye to my family once again. I am glad I got to share this day with them.

This Spring day in April is turning out to be a hot day. The temperature high for the day climbs to the lower 90's. My friend John commits to run with me to the edge of Tulsa. We leave Tracy Park and head east along 11th street.

John runs down Route 66 with me for the next three hot hours. We will run a couple miles and then rest in the shade of our Winnebago with Bud and Dan. We have police cruisers escorting us through Tulsa. The motorcycle escort is gone.

During one of our rest stops, one of the police officers providing escort, presented me an honorary Tulsa Police Department badge. It isn't the metal type of badge, but a stick on. It is my first honorary badge I have acquired during my run and I don't care from what material it was made. The officer peals off the adhesive backing and slaps it on my chest. I have a badge. This is cool!

We run all the way together in the heat to the eastern edge of the Tulsa City limits near 193rd East Avenue. John gives me a hug, wishes me well, and thanks me for giving him the opportunity to run.

This is John Swasho's "Always Walking" story regarding his opportunity to run with me.

"When I had been invited to run with my friend Steve, I jumped at the opportunity. I didn't realize what I had signed up for. Besides the benefit of a good workout, I gained the gift of vision. The type of vision it takes to set a goal and accomplish it. My friend taught me, not always by words, that this type of feat more time than not means drawing on the strength and courage that only comes from above. Steve also gave me the gift of looking beyond the boundaries and limits of my own imagination in which I started to pray and believe. I really broaden my prayer and faith to include those that were benefiting from what Steve was doing by running for Special Olympics.

I ran across the city limits of Tulsa with Steve, and was inspired by the start of the Tulsa leg, where Steve was greeted with smiles, hugs, and cheers from others. We were then escorted by the Tulsa Police motorcade as we ran alone old Route 66, with some passersby encouraging and some thinking we were crazy for running in the heat of the day on 120 degree pavement. As I left Steve on the eastern outskirts of Tulsa near Catoosa, it was hard to leave my friend because I knew he was more than road weary. He was beat up by the previous ten days of running. But I remembered what Steve shared with me and that is we all have something to contribute, something to do, something to give of ourselves."

John has left me, and once again it's time to run alone. I enjoyed his company for the past few hours. His companionship helped me get through the heat and the miles.

I continue running for another hour until I reach Catoosa. My knee is hurting once again, so I decide this is a good stopping point for the day. When your hot, tired and your knees don't want to work anymore, it's time meet up the my support team Bud and Dan.

We end the day with a reception at the Ramada Inn located on Admiral street in Tulsa. It is a surprise party for me and my support team. Our new friend Wanda Shanks, the Manager of the Ramada, put together a surprise reception that would bring Special Olympic athletes of Catoosa together with Forrest Gump. Dan, Bud and myself are guests of honor at a reception at the hotel. We meet with a dozen Special Olympic athletes, and the three of us share our experiences with them.

Pizza and a cake are presented which included white icing and the words Run Forrest Run. The reception is an opportunity for these Special Olympics athletes and their families to meet us and say thank you. We spend the next hour and a half visiting, taking photographs and eating! I am encouraged by the kind words and well wishes of the Special Olympic athletes.

Like so many times before, it is time to say thank you and good-bye. This good-bye is a little different. I will see these athletes the next day when I run through the city of Catoosa and visit their school.

Today, was a good day. It was good to be home in Tulsa. It was a hot day for a run, but sometimes you have to do a difficult thing to make a difference. Today, I felt like I made a difference! I end the day exhausted, but feeling good about what has been accomplished.

I'm sad because my good friend Dan Miyoshi will be leaving the support team and heading back home to Las Vegas tomorrow. I will miss Dan immensely. He has provided not only physical support, but tremendous emotional support for the past five days. He has always been one of my favorites. Dan is a true friend and I am honored to know him.

Dan wrote a few words in my journal and this is what he had to say.

"Steve, At this hour there are only two people awake here in the Ramada. You, with your soft knee, and me, with my soft heart. I know we could both be doing much worse. I wish that there could have been more for me to give to this worthy cause. Will try harder in the future. There is so much to remember from this trek. From the declaration of "Steve Kime Day" on the south steps, my first tears of the week, to the pizza party tonight, what I hope to be the last tears of the week. It seems to me that in this world we all face certain challenges in life, as well as the seeds of greatness. The true measure of a man or woman is to be found not only in his ability to overcome these challenges, but also in his ability to assist others to attain greatness. Thank you for sharing so much with so many."

Lesson #12: Give back to others each and every day. So many people have given of themselves over the past several days. From providing a cup of water, for providing an escort of protection, and for providing companionship. I am reminded of a quote from Kahill Gibran who once said, "You truly give when you give of yourself." Remember, a life lived for others is the life worthwhile.

APRIL 10, 2001

The day has arrived that I will meet my friends from Cherokee Elementary and Helen Paul grade school of Catoosa. Donna Tapley, from Cherokee Elementary has called me periodically to check on my progress as I run across the state. She would call me on my cell phone and ask how I was feeling. I would give her my medical update on the knees and the status of my blisters. Donna also ask me to confirm that I would be arriving in Catoosa on the morning of April 10th. Little did I know what the students at all three schools in Catoosa had in store for me. I admire Donna and her sincere efforts to check on me during my run across the state.

I thought, "how nice of her to keep checking on me." All the while, she was making sure that the "guest of honor" would still be standing when he arrived in Catoosa. I just didn't know that I was the "guest of honor."

I begin the morning at the football stadium at Catoosa High School, home of the Indians. I run out onto the track inside the stadium, along with the Catoosa Special Olympic athletes. With these athletes by my side, I share with the balance of the students the importance of following their dreams. I share briefly some highlights of my run thus far across the state, but emphasize the importance of pursuing one's dreams.

I am encouraged by the opportunity to address the hundreds of students. This is more than Steve running across the state. It is an opportunity for me to be an exhorter. I want to be a source of encouragement to all I meet along Route 66.

After a brief photo session, I am off and running on the Mother Road. I am told that our next stop, Cherokee Elementary, is about one mile away. I'm running northeast with my final destination tonight of Chelsea, Oklahoma. I am excited about this part of the run because I know that I'm about two thirds the way done with my run. The Kansas state line is only days away.

About two city blocks from Cherokee Elementary and Helen Paul school, I see that Route 66 is lined on both sides by students holding yellow, round smiley face signs that have "Run Forrest Run" printed on them. These hundreds of bright yellow smiley faces is a sight that brings tears to my eyes. Believe me, it's difficult to run, smile and act cool, while all the time you're trying to hold back tears. I am so overwhelmed with emotions at this point, I feel no pain. The knees and the blisters don't matter. The "guest of honor" was running down Route 66, right in the middle of shouts of joy from the students. Now, I know why Ms.Tapley kept checking on me. These students have been waiting for my arrival for twelve days.

I run down the east side of the road, giving the students the "high five" slap as I run by. As I run out of students, I turn and run back south along the west side of Route 66. More "high five" slaps and more tears for me to hide. After I complete the run in front of the school, I am stopped and asked if I would run around the track located on the playground area behind the school. At first, I have this selfish thought of, "you want me to run an extra quarter-mile around the track after I've been running for 200 miles?" Then I realize once again, this is more than a Steve run. Not the time to be selfish. It's an opportunity to touch the lives of hundreds of students, parents and faculty members.

I say yes and off we go. We run along side of the school and enter the track area. We decide to run in a clock-wise direction, and I'm surrounded by hundreds of fourth and fifth graders. I keep thinking of how I could have used their companionship the previous 200 miles. What a thrill for me to be surrounded by these energetic students, who were having the most fun by running with Forrest.

After running around the track one time, I stop and thank the students for being there for me. They encouraged me so much this morning. What goes around comes around. Earlier this morning I'm encouraging high schools students to make good choices, stay in school and follow their dreams. Now, I have these grade school students encouraging me.

As I am leaving the school, my wife Debbie tells me a student in a wheel chair wants to meet me. His name is Matthew and this fourth grade student is unable to run with us around the playground due to his confinement to a wheel chair. But, that didn't stop him from making a yellow smiley face sign for me. I pose with Matthew, we take a few photos, I autograph a smiley face sign and give it to him. He in turn, has already written on his sign and gives it to me. This is what this run across the state is all about. Touching other people's lives and being touched in return.

I had the privilege of going back to Cherokee Elementary eleven months later to visit with my friends. It was nice to have a brief reunion with my encouragers. I was given the opportunity to thank each of them once again for their support and for making all of those yellow smiley face signs. I shared with them my five minute video that encompasses the sixteen day run. During the video, there is a segment on the tape that shows all the students running with me. It brought back a flood of memories for both these students and myself.

I leave the elementary school and continue down Route 66, but within just a few hundred feet I meet up with the grade school kids from Helen Paul school. They greet me with a big sign that was autographed by many of the students. These young pre-school kids don't want a "high-five" slap of hands. They want a hug. I am so moved by their innocent desire to just hug me. As far as they are concerned, I am Forrest Gump and am taking time to jog by their school. One of my favorite photos in my collection of memories is when I'm standing in front of the Helen Paul School with four students hugging me. Once again, these students standing along side Route 66 waiting for me to pass by, stir my heart with emotion. Before I leave my new grade school friends, I'm presented with a bouquet of helium filled balloons and gracious words of well-wishes.

This day has contained the full spectrum of emotions for me. I am overwhelmed with love, concern, compassion and friendship during my visits to three schools.

So, it's me and my good friend Bud. He has been with me since day one. Bud keeps telling me he's having the time of his life. I think we all pursue days like today.

Bud leaves in our Winnebago on Route 66, and stops five miles down the road and waits. In the meantime, a member of the Catoosa police department escorts me through the remainder of the city. I run along the east side of Route 66 and stop just across from the notorious Blue Whale.

I think most people in northeastern Oklahoma have heard of the Blue Whale on the northern edge of Catoosa. Floating in a rather murky pond of water is a blue whale that has served as recreation to swimmers in this once popular tourist stop. I've heard that in the early days, you could swim in the pond and dive off or slide down various parts of the whale. Like the fading color of the blue whale, this is just one more historical landmark along Route 66 that is fading into history.

We take a few moments to reminisce about the events that we just witnessed at the schools.

Before he leaves me, and since I can't run with my helium-filled balloons, the officer suggests I write a note and tie it to the bouquet. We say a few more words of appreciation and let the balloons lift away. The Blue Whale to my left, the Mother Road in front, and balloons traveling skyward, it's time to run. Next city on our stop will be Claremore.

This is a story from Shelley Gibson, Special Education Teacher and Special Olympic coach at Catoosa High School.

"I was so excited when I heard that Forrest Gump (Steve Kime) would be running through Catoosa. I explained to my high school athletes about his dream and they immediately wanted to be a part of this historic event. The news quickly spread around the district that Forrest would be stopping here on April 10, 2001. The day before this event, a woman from the Ramada Inn in Tulsa contacted me. She explained to me that Forrest (Steve) and his crew would be

staying there that night and wanted to know if I would like to participate in a surprise reception for them. We discussed what we would like to do and then each of us made phone calls. I met Wanda and my athletes about 30 minutes before Steve and crew was to arrive to decorate the room. After this task was finished, we anxiously awaited in the lobby area to surprise Steve. This was actually the first time I was able to think about what we were doing. He was doing something for all the Special Olympics athletes and now it was our turn to do something special for him. I will always remember the look on Steve's face when he came around the corner and saw all the athletes there to greet him. It was an unforgettable sight! After taking pictures, we made our way to the reception were Steve said a few words to the athletes. His words made me realize how important our small efforts were. He said that this was the first time that a group of athletes had met him at the hotel and that day he was feeling down and sore, but our group had given him encouragement needed to finish his run across Route 66.

The following day, Steve stopped at Catoosa High School to share his dream with the students. He encouraged the students to follow your dream no matter what. I will always remember those words. He made our Special Olympic athletes feel very important that day. He helped show to the other students how special these athletes really are. Because of his efforts, we had many high school students volunteer to help with Special Olympics.

I will always remember the Route 66 run because it proves that anyone can accomplish their dreams. Catoosa High School Special Olympic athletes will always remember the day they met Forrest Gump!"

Well, it's Bud and me for the rest of the way to the Kansas state line. Bud is leading the way to our next scheduled stop, which is the city of Claremore. I've grown to really respect and appreciate Bud for his unselfish work on behalf of Special Olympic athletes and for all the support he has provided me.

It's an overcast sky but the temperature is rather pleasant for a run. My knee continues to bother me so I do a lot of running and race walking, working my way north on Route 66. I'm determined to get the miles in today, beside I've got a lot of ribs to eat tonight!

We are scheduled to meet this evening with a Special Olympic baseball team from Claremore. The restaurant in which we are meeting is well know for it's great ribs.

I start receiving phone calls from one Special Olympic parent who lives in Claremore. She has seen some of the Tulsa television new stories about my run across the state, and is excited I will be running through her hometown. When Judy learned I would be running through Claremore on Tuesday, she called me and asked if it would be all right if her son and a friend could join me. I said, "Yes, I would certainly enjoy the company."

I'm going as fast as I can heading towards Claremore knowing that two special individuals will join me. I work my way into the south edge of the city and I am met by a group of five people who include my two new Special Olympics friends named Stephanie and Nathan. We meet at the edge of the Walmart parking lot and exchange hello's. I meet Judy and it's good to put a face with the phone calls I have received. It is an exciting time for Bud, my new friends and myself. They are joining my run at a time when I need the companionship and encouragement.

We spend the majority of the time race walking down Route 66 which goes right through the middle of downtown Claremore. If you're in Claremore, Route 66 is also known as the Will Rogers Highway. I share my stories and experiences from my previous days running along the Mother Road with Stephanie and Nathan. They seem impressed that I was able to cover all those miles on foot, but I think they are more impressed to see that I am just an ordinary guy that is pursuing a dream. We spend the next few hours together and we learn a lot about each other. I learn that these two Special Olympic athletes have many dreams to experience and I believe they learned from me that when you put a PLAN in place, you can live the dream.

My new friend Nathan Willhoite made these observations during our time together in Claremore.

"Walking with you made me feel famous and proud. Almost as proud as when I make a play at third base. Seeing cars going by, and people looking at us and wondering what

are we doing and how did Forrest get out of the movie to be in my hometown, Claremore. Also, going to my job at Warehouse Market with you and meeting my friends was like a dream come true, not to mention the party we had at the Rib Crib, and sharing the wonderful cake with Forrest and my baseball team.

Thank you Steve, thank you Forrest for that day you made my Mom so happy and my Dad so happy."

Bud and I end that day at the south end of Foyil city limits, home of the great Andy Payne.

Lesson #13: Life is a school. There are many teachers. We just need to participate in life and let the learning begin! Remember, school is never out!

APRIL 11, 2001

B ud and I are excited about the beginnings of today, because we are the guests of the Chelsea Grade School. We are the honored guest of hundreds of first, second and third grade classes. It is pouring down rain that morning, but doesn't dampen our spirits at all. These children are so excited to see us. Again, it is warming to our hearts to be hugged and greeted by all of these precious children.

I am presented with a "box of chocolates" and handed a large handmade "Welcome" poster. The poster is autographed by all the students and the word "welcome" has enough glitter to cover the state of Oklahoma. I have forgotten how "cool" it is to work with glue and glitter.

The students sing a few songs and present a rather enthusiastic cheer to us. These students are so thoughtful. After their presentation, I think, "this is just one more reason for running across the state. It gives these students an opportunity to give back to their school, to their community and to me. These grade school students have been waiting on me for thirteen days to arrive in Chelsea. The students and faculty really know how to throw a welcome party!

The brief morning at school and spending time with those students will always be a highlight of my run down the Mother Road.

Since we arrived in Foyil late Tuesday night, and we had the "rib" dinner engagement with the Special Olympics athletes back in

Claremore, we didn't have time to visit a special monument that is dedicated to a special Cherokee Indian. I want to make sure that we visit the Andy Payne statue just off Route 66.

In 1928, Andy won the world famous International Transcontinental Foot Marathon. Three and a-half months and three thousand four hundred twenty two miles later, Andy was the winner of the foot race that the media labeled the Bunion Derby. This was a cross-country foot race that started in California and traveled along Route 66 all the way to Chicago. From the Windy City, the race continued on to Madison Square Garden in New York. Seeing the statue of Andy really gave a perspective of the significance of his achievement. Imagine, running over three thousand miles all in an effort to win some money. I read that Andy used his first place winnings and paid off the debt of the family farm. Andy Payne must have been a very special person.

I pose next to the statue of Andy and Bud takes a few pictures, all the while thinking about what type of person would be willing to run across the United States. I thought my feat of running across Oklahoma was significant, but running from California to New York, now that's an accomplishment. I start to recall some of my challenges and pleasant memories during my run across the state, and I wonder about the challenges and memories that greeted Andy as he ran across the country.

I leave the statue of Andy and the city of Foyil behind and head northeast to Vinita. I think of this special place on Route 66 with tremendous admiration for all those runners who attempted to run across this great country. I know for a fact that it takes a physically fit body and the utmost determination to run for the prize.

Lesson #14: Hug your kids today! I will always remember the unconditional love and hugs I received from the little children at Helen Paul School from the previous day and from the students at Chelsea grade school. Their actions reminded the importance of giving hugs willingly. "Give a little love to a child, and you get a great deal back."—John Ruskin

Thursday

APRIL 12, 2001

Our goal today is to get from Vinita to Miami. It is a rather warm, humid spring day. Typical Oklahoma weather for a day in April. The clearest of blue skies and the wide open Route 66 roadway in front of us. I notice that Bud my teammate is getting a little tired at this point of the trip. Besides the responsibility of driving the Winnebago and signing my name to the credit card gas purchases, Bud has been responsible for all on-the-road public relations. I couldn't have asked for a better PR Manager. Bud is an expert on the cell phone, and can locate any police officer, newspaper reporter, and any interested by-stander from miles away. He is always getting the word out to the next community on our route, that Forrest is just a few miles away. Bud is such a "conversationalist" and reminds me of Will Rogers. After spending about fourteen days with Bud, I learned that just like Will, he "never met a man he didn't like."

Numerous times Bud was a photojournalist. As I mentioned, we videotaped the run across the Main Street of America. Bud became very proficient in running the camera and helping me stage some of the pictorial events. Many times as I would be running, I would cross a bridge or run down a stretch of Route 66 that needed to be captured on videotape. Whether it's a street lined with people, an old 75 year old bridge that use to allow Model A's to cross, or while running down the brownish portland cement surface in western Oklahoma, it was important to record.

I think Bud enjoyed this role as a photographer as we made our way across the state. The still photography shots and most of the video takes were taken by Bud. I appreciate him recording this event, which allows many of us to enjoy playing back the video and browsing through the photo album to this day. If there ever was an Ambassador for my run across the state, that job belonged to Bud. He has become a true friend!

As we continue northeastward, this was just a day to get the miles in. A rather non eventful day, but at least the extraordinary clear blue Oklahoma sky greeted us as we worked our way down Route 66 to Miami, Oklahoma. After arriving in Afton, we reach a segment of the Mother Road that is about nine feet wide. It is paved with the brownish Portland Cement that is so common in the western part of Oklahoma.

This stretch of Route 66 is barely wide enough for two Model T's to pass each other. When I arrive at this noted section of the road, I am disappointed to find that the Oklahoma County Highway crew has spread rock and gravel on top of the surface. Besides making it dangerous and difficult for me to run, the rock they sprayed covered up the surface of the infamous Portland concrete. Finding this portion of the Mother Road covered by gravel, ruined another photo opportunity.

Bud leads the way, cell phone in one hand, video camera in the other, while commandeering our home away from home, the Winnebago. For me, I do what I've been doing for the past fifteen days, and that is just keep running.

> **Lesson #15: "The only way to have a friend is to be one."—Ralph Waldo Emerson**
> **Bud was a great example of being a friend. Mile after mile, he was always there to lend a helping hand. I will follow his example of true friendship with those individuals in my life.**

Friday

APRIL 13, 2001

I start the morning leaving the Best Western Motel with a run through downtown Miami. I am escorted by a police Officer all the way to the historic Coleman Theatre. I am greeted by the Miami Chamber of Commerce officials, a writer and photographer from the Tulsa World newspaper, a television crew from Joplin, Missouri and four young high schools girls that are members of the local track team.

I also meet up with a young man named John Allemann. I met John six months earlier during my run across Kansas. I mentioned to several individuals during the run across Kansas, that in April the following year I would be running across Oklahoma. John was one individual that remembered my comment and followed my run across the state through various e-mails. I am pleasantly surprised to see John and I am impressed that he even recalled this feat.

After a few interviews and presentations inside the restored lobby of the Coleman Theatre, it is time to run. Now, I'm heading for the Kansas border and the finish line. I've been waiting for this day a long time. Standing outside the theatre is a group of four young ladies from the Miami track team and their parents. As I venture out onto the street, I am asked by the father of one of the girls if it would be alright if they ran with me a few miles. I said, "I would love the company." So many of the miles across the state were done in solitude. I welcomed the opportunity to visit while running. We run about one mile before the girls have to leave. We had a great visit and they enjoyed their "fifteen minutes" of fame by running with Forrest.

In the Saturday edition of the Tulsa World, there is a colorful photograph and caption that shows John, the four girls and myself running down Route 66 on the edge of Miami. We say our farewells to each other and now it's just myself, my friend John plus fifteen miles to the state line.

I have a new support team as this time. My friend Bud had to return to Oklahoma City last night, so my new help mates are Mike and Carol Brumley. Mike and Carol admit they are new at this support role, but are ready to escort me to the finish at the Kansas border.

Only fifteen miles left of my 397-mile run. Piece of cake! The excitement from the festivities at the Coleman Theatre earlier this morning and the company of a few extra runners help get my mind off my painful knees. John takes control of the conversation while we run, and I just mumble something in acknowledgement. He asked me about the events across the state and it gives me a chance to reminisce and share some of the highlights. I am really enjoying the company these last few miles.

We enter the town of Commerce, home of New York Yankee Mickey Mantle, and are escorted through the city by a local police officer. The only excitement we encountered while running through town is being chased by a big black dog on the edge of city limits. I guess this dog is protecting his section of the Mother Road, because he does not like the fact that John and I are in his territory. You would think after 390 miles I would be used to dogs chasing me. Not so! To this day, I still feel the terror when I see those dogs dart out and chase me.

John and I keep running toward the border. We pass through the city of Quapaw, which is about five miles from the state line. As we're running through town there is a gas and food store situated on Route 66 that has a marquis with the message: "Quapaw Express – Welcome and Thanks Steve Kime—Running for Special Olympics." The townspeople were so excited that Forrest was going to run through their city, and they rolled out the welcome mat to us with these messages on the marquis.

It felt good to see my name on the sign, but it felt even better when I saw the words Special Olympics. I am thrilled to know that the run is to benefit Special Olympics and everyone realized that to be the case. We take a few photos and I'm anxious to get this run done!

At the north edge of Quapaw is a green rectangle shaped highway sign that says, "State Line Five Miles." At this point, I actually believe that I'm going to finish. After all these days of running, the end is in sight! I think I can finish this run in a vertical position and somewhat conscious. Some people say the first step is the toughest when going forward. I'm here to say the last five miles of a 397-mile run is the toughest. I don't know if someone put that state sign in the wrong place, but that was the longest five miles to run. I kept asking John, "Is this really five miles? I don't recall a mile being this long."

From about one mile away, we can see the Winnebago parked off the shoulder of the road. That's it! The finish, the state line is in sight! I am familiar with this part of Route 66 and the Kansas State Line.

My left knee continues to scream at me in tremendous pain. But, with my focus on the finish, I'm not listening to it. I see Carol and her husband Mike standing by the Winnebago with camera in hand. I see three or four other individuals standing along side the Brumley's, but I don't recognize them. I'm about 100 yards from the finish and I notice this photographer from the Tulsa World, whom I met at Miami's Coleman Theatre earlier that morning, laying down on the shoulder of the road. I later saw in the next day Saturday edition of the Tulsa World, this photographer took the photograph from that angle, to capture my state line finish. It was such an unusual sight to see this guy laying down on his side with camera aimed in my direction. Doesn't matter to me, I keep running along with my friend John and we cross the Kansas State Line. It is finished!

At 2:10pm, on Good Friday, April 13, 2001, I completed my 397-mile run across Oklahoma on "The Main Street of America." I will forever look at Route 66 in a different way. Now, there is a personal connection to the Mother Road. Today, when I drive down

Route 66, an avalanche of memories overtake me. The run, the people, the pain, the joys, have changed me in many ways.

After a few interviews with reporters from the Baxter Springs, Kansas newspapers, it's time to say good-bye. I say farewell to the reporters, to my friend John, to the Quapaw police officer who provided the escort, and to the State Line.

Just like the start some sixteen days ago, there was no fanfare or bands playing when I crossed the state line. No celebrations! No large crowds to watch the finish. Sometimes we play over and over a scene in our minds on how they would play out. During the run, I didn't think much about the finish line festivities, but I did think about the finish. I thought often of what it would feel like to reach the border and stop running. No more pain to the knees or to my feet. Those pain free thoughts and to experience the crossing of the finish line was celebration enough for me.

It's time to go home. I get on the Winnebago with my support team members Mike and Carol, and we head for Tulsa. Back down Route 66. This time I'm riding, riding down the Main Street of America.

Lesson #16: Go the distance! Dreams still come true.

FINAL WORDS

Since the beginning of this writing project, several months have passed. Recently I received some sad news regarding my friend Ashley Alexander. My friend who waved at me from his front yard garden as I was running to Bill's Corner passed away. His death has reminded me about the briefness of life. I guess now, Ashley will be working in his heavenly garden and will be waving at me from above. I can still see him today with his radiant smile and a countenance of joy on his face. Ashley my friend, you will be missed!

One of my favorite movies is entitled: *The Shawshank Redemption.* The story is about a young man in prison and how he dealt with his life sentence in this maximum facility without any hopes for parole. He received this undeserving sentence for a crime he did not commit. A scene in the movie that has made a lasting impression on me shows this prisoner and his friend sitting on the ground with their backs up against a cold, hard rock wall. They talked about the *"what ifs"* in life. *"What if"* this would have happened and *"what if"* I had done that and *"what if"* I went this way? Finally, after a few minutes of deep reflection on the turns of life they both experienced, the prisoner in prison for a crime he did not commit tells his friend in a philosophical manner, *"You know, it just comes down to this. You either get busy livin' or get busy dying. I choose to live!"* Later in the movie, the prisoner escapes from prison after years spent planning his timely departure.

So, it's time to get busy. It's time to work your P.L.A.N. and live your dream. If you have reached this point in the book, you definitely mean business. Congratulations, you're on your way! Nothing is going to stop you now. Not even those big dogs that might come chasing after you. Live the Dream! Go for it! Life is a series of choices. Some good, and some not so good. You are making a choice to make a difference. At this very moment, you are making a choice to make a difference in your life and in the lives of those you touch. As you live your dream, you will touch many people. Follow your heart and enjoy the ride. You have a divine appointment with a dream.

Got to run! Wishing you the best my friend! Sweet dreams!

ABOUT THE AUTHOR

Steve Kime, is an award winning radio broadcaster, a "record setting" athlete and Fortune 100 corporate trainer. Steve is known as an encourager and motivator. Today, he continues to encourage audiences with his motivational messages that "make the difference."

Steve was active in all sports and set individual and team track records. Steve attended college on a track scholarship and graduated from the University of Oklahoma and from Elkins Institute of Broadcasting in Oklahoma City. During his broadcasting career, Steve produced two radio commercials that were voted "Best Radio Commercials" in the state of Oklahoma and for which he was presented an award by the Oklahoma Broadcasters Association.

Steve is President of Steve Kime and Associates. A Tulsa, Oklahoma based company that provides personal development seminars to individuals and corporations. The seminars focus on helping people "reach their full potential" both on a personal and professional level. He is a member of the American Society of Training and Development and the National Speakers Association.

Steve is the author of the book entitled: *How Will They Remember Me?* He has also written articles that have been published in national periodicals.

To contact Steve Kime write to:
P.O. Box 52552
Tulsa, Oklahoma 74152-0552
Tel. (918) 747-9076
e-mail: kimespeakr@aol.com
or visit www.SteveKime.com

A WORD ABOUT SPECIAL OLYMPICS OKLAHOMA

Special Olympics Oklahoma is a year-round sports training and athletic competition program for people with mental retardation. Special Olympics was founded by Eunice Kennedy Shriver in 1968. Currently, over 8,000 athletes participate in 17 official sports across Oklahoma. Annually, there are over 100 state, area, and local events, over 1,700 volunteer coaches, and nearly 11,000 annual volunteer opportunities. For more information about becoming a Special Olympics Oklahoma athlete, programs in your area, training, coaching, sponsoring, or volunteering please call (918) 481-1234. www.sook.org

SPONSORS THANK YOU

A special note of thanks goes to the sponsors of my run across Oklahoma. Cingular Wireless; Conoco; Dollar Rent A Car; Eskimo Joe's with the design of a commemorative 75th Anniversary Route 66 T Shirt; Avcom Productions; Lewis RV for my home away from home, plus my friend Bob Hoenig of Runners World, and Townsend Marketing, Inc. Thank you all!

Lesson #15: "The only way to have a friend is to be one."—Ralph Waldo Emerson

Bud was a great example of being a friend. Mile after mile, he was always there to lend a helping hand. I will follow his example of true friendship with those individuals in my life.

Lesson #16: Go the distance! Dreams still come true.

Printed in the United States
1084900005B/199-243

9 781591 605539

"Steve Kime is a very special person. I realized this the day he told me he was going to run across Oklahoma. Now, Oklahoma is a very wide state, and I asked Steve if he wouldn't rather do the Oklahoma Panhandle first.

"No, he persisted, he planned to cross the whole state and do it in 16 days in order to raise awareness of and funds for Special Olympics. He did it, too!

"I've always believed when we reach out to help others, we are touching the hand of God, and Steve Kime is doing that every day. His is a must-read book. Steve is my hero."

—Tom Harken—
WINNER OF THE 1992 HORATIO ALGER AWARD
and Author of The Millionaire's Secret

❖

"Get off the bench and in the game of life. Read this profound book!"

—Rudy Ruettiger—
TOP MOTIVATIONAL SPEAKER
Author, and the inspiration behind the TriStar hit movie Rudy

❖

"There are some people that have more than a dream or a goal to attain. They are the few that have a call on their lives who are at specific places, at specific times, with words and actions that change people's lives. This story shows a man fulfilling his personal call and destiny on the behalf of many. The journey becomes the process in which he achieves his purpose, completes his assignment, and looks intensely at what lies ahead."

—Madeline Manning Mims—
FOUR-TIME OLYMPIAN,
GOLD AND SILVER MEDALIST
Author of The Hope of Glory

STEVE KIME is a professional speaker who encourages audiences across the country to make a difference! Steve is an award-winning radio broadcaster and "record-setting" athlete.

Steve is President of Steve Kime and Associates, a Tulsa, Oklahoma-based company that provides personal development seminars to individuals and corporations. The seminars focus on helping people "reach their full potential," both on personal and professional levels.

ISBN 1-591605-53-9

Xulon PRESS

9 781591 605539
90000

LESSONS

Lesson #1: Keep your head and heart going in the right direction and you will not have to worry about your feet. This is fun, living the dream!

Lesson #2: When someone hands you cash money, or when someone offers their hand— take it! Seriously, I was moved by the generosity of this man and also of the many individuals that stopped and offered help. In a time when we are so busy going from point A to B, it was refreshing to know there are people that are willing to stop, go out of their way, and be of assistance. I am reminded that I need to slow down, take the time to help others, even if it means stopping or going out of my way.

Lesson #3: The objective is the same, but the strategy can change. I also learned the valuable lesson of having someone in your life that you can share your heart with. As you pursue your dream, it's important to always have someone 'in your corner" that will offer a word of encouragement and wisdom.

Lesson #4: You can't outrun the big dogs so keep a hubcap close by. Seriously, we will face various forms of weather as we pursue the dream. The wind will not always be at our back, and the sun may not always shine in our favor, but with a strong sense of direction and purpose, one will prevail.

Lesson #5: Life's little opportunities to offer a word of encouragement come in many different ways. Whether it's showing up at a boy's baseball team practice, visiting with a next door neighbor, or crossing paths with a perfect stranger, God has a way of bringing people into our lives that need to hear a word of inspiration. Take a moment today and look for "life's opportunities" to encourage one another.

Lesson #6: Life is a series of choices. Choices to do good or to do bad. A choice to offer kindness or to offer nothing. This young man made a conscious choice to help and to offer assistance to me a perfect stranger. How many people do you know are willing to take a moment out of their day to help another. I will always remember his kind deed, and his outstretched hand, which reminds me that I too should make the choice to help a perfect stranger.

Lesson #7: It's important to follow your dreams even if others do not believe in you! Not everyone may view things the same way. The vast majority of people I met during my sixteen day run were very supportive and accommodating. A few individuals did not share the same enthusiasm. I learned today, not everyone will agree with my dream or desires and goals. I recall the old English proverb that says, "Keep company with those that may make you better."

Lesson #8: When you can, do something to make your "momma" proud! What a thrill, surprise and honor to receive a Proclamation Day in my honor. I hope to be able to give back to Oklahoma and Special Olympics and be worthy of this honor. I am reminded of this quote by Pierre Charron. "He who receives a benefit should never forget it; he who bestows should never remember it."

Lesson #9: Do whatever you can to build and nurture your support system. With the support of family and friends, how can anyone not achieve their dreams?

Lesson #10: As we hurry down life's highway, take a few moments to help another along the way. The gracious bikers taught me something new about giving. Even though they were on a "mission" to get to Oklahoma City, they took the time to help us with the cause.

Lesson #11: It is a great education and incredible experience to see things during our travels. I think it is important for individuals to travel and see how the world lives. There is something comforting about coming home. A safe place that you call your own. There's no place like home. You're right Dorothy, there's no place like home.

Lesson #12: Give back to others each and every day. So many people have given of themselves over the past several days. From providing a cup of water, for providing an escort of protection, and for providing companionship. I am reminded of a quote from Kahill Gibran who once said, "You truly give when you give of yourself." Remember, a life lived for others is the life worthwhile.

Lesson #13: Life is a school. There are many teachers. We just need to participate in life and let the learning begin! Remember, school is never out!

Lesson #14: Hug your kids today! I will always remember the unconditional love and hugs I received from the little children at Helen Paul School from the previous day and from the students at Chelsea grade school. Their actions reminded the importance of giving hugs willingly. "Give a little love to a child, and you get a great deal back."—John Ruskin